SWEET VALLEY TWINS

◇ SUPER CHILLER ◇

The Secret of the Magic Pen

◇

Written by
Jamie Suzanne

LOCAL

BANTAM BOOKS
NEW YORK · TORONTO · LONDON · SYDNEY · AUCKLAND

THE SECRET OF THE MAGIC PEN
A BANTAM BOOK : 0 553 50317 0

Originally published in USA by Bantam Books

First publication in Great Britain

PRINTING HISTORY
Bantam edition published 1996

The trademarks "Sweet Valley" and "Sweet Valley Twins"
are owned by Francine Pascal and are used under license by
Bantam Books and Transworld Publishers Ltd.

Conceived by Francine Pascal.

Produced by Daniel Weiss Associates, Inc,
33 West 17th Street, New York, NY 10011

All rights reserved.

Copyright © 1995 by Francine Pascal

Cover photo by Oliver Hunter

Bantam Books are published by Transworld Publishers Ltd,
61–63 Uxbridge Road, Ealing, London W5 5SA,
in Australia by Transworld Publishers (Australia) Pty Ltd,
15–25 Helles Avenue, Moorebank, NSW 2170,
and in New Zealand by Transworld Publishers (NZ) Ltd,
3 William Pickering Drive, Albany, Auckland.

Printed and bound in Great Britain by
Cox & Wyman Ltd, Reading, Berkshire.

To Daniel Henry Marks

One

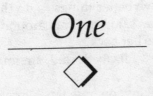

There's nothing better than a good mystery, Elizabeth Wakefield thought after she read the final page of Amanda Howard's latest novel. The beginning was always intriguing, the middle was frightening, and the end was unpredictable. Elizabeth clutched the book affectionately as she leaned back in her desk chair.

"Hi." Elizabeth's twin sister, Jessica, stuck her head through the doorway. "Done with that boring book yet?"

Elizabeth sighed. "First of all, the book wasn't at all boring. It was fabulous—I had no idea who the killer was until the very end."

Jessica stepped into the room and began adjusting her purple bikini in front of the full-length mirror.

"And second of all," Elizabeth continued, "you wouldn't know even if it *was* boring, because you've never read a single Amanda Howard mystery."

"Well, I have better things to do than read mysteries," Jessica said, turning around so that she could examine her back.

"Oh, yeah?" Elizabeth said, smiling. "Like what better things?"

"Like working on my tan," Jessica answered. "Now, put on a swimsuit and come down to the pool with me."

"Go ahead without me. I'm just about to start writing a story of my own." Elizabeth took a blank pad out of the drawer. "Amanda Howard has inspired me."

"You're no fun," Jessica complained.

"I think we just have different ideas about what fun is," Elizabeth replied.

Elizabeth and Jessica Wakefield may have had the same long, sun-streaked blond hair, sparkling blue-green eyes, and dimples in their left cheeks, but they definitely had different ideas about how to survive a hot summer in Sweet Valley.

Fun for Jessica meant anything involving boys, clothes, or the Unicorn Club. The Unicorn Club was an exclusive group consisting of the prettiest and most popular girls at Sweet Valley Middle School. Elizabeth had been asked to be a member, too, but she felt that nothing sounded less interesting than hanging around with the snootiest girls in Sweet Valley. Jessica, on the other hand, adored attending the weekly meetings, gossiping with her fellow members, and dressing in purple, the official club color. As long as the Unicorns were around, there seemed to be an endless supply of good times.

Elizabeth's idea of fun was simpler and quieter than her sister's. She loved curling up with an Amanda Howard mystery, having long talks with friends, and writing articles for *The Sweet Valley Sixers*, the class newspaper she had helped found.

But despite their differences, the Wakefield twins were the best of friends.

Jessica sat down on the edge of Elizabeth's bed with a groan. "I could just kill Lila for jetting off to Europe with her father for the summer." Lila, Jessica's best friend after Elizabeth, was the daughter of the richest man in Sweet Valley. "At this very moment she's probably sunbathing on an island in Greece. Or shopping for a new wardrobe in Paris. Or licking a gigantic gelato in Italy. And she didn't even invite me!" Jessica flopped dramatically on the bed.

"I know what you mean," Elizabeth said with a sigh. "I'm getting a little bored, too. Amy's always studying—I've hardly seen her all summer." Elizabeth's best friend, Amy Sutton, had been accepted to a prestigious summer school program in Sweet Valley. "Maybe I should have signed up with her. I could have taken a creative writing course."

"Practically all the Unicorns are doing something fun this summer," Jessica continued. "Yesterday, Ellen Riteman went to visit her grandmother in Wyoming."

Elizabeth raised an eyebrow. "I didn't realize that Wyoming was your kind of place."

"Well, at least it's a change of scenery," Jessica responded.

Elizabeth nodded. "And Todd's probably having the time of his life at sports camp." Todd Wilkins was Elizabeth's sort-of boyfriend.

"I'm so bored I wish it was time to go back to school," Jessica declared.

Elizabeth giggled at her sister's unlikely comment. "You don't miss class, Jess. You just miss eating lunch in the Unicorner and having a locker near Aaron Dallas."

"And Rick Hunter," Jessica added dreamily.

"There must be *something* fun we can do," Elizabeth mused.

"Everything there is to do in Sweet Valley, we've done at least a million and one times," Jessica reminded her twin.

"Yeah, I guess you're right," Elizabeth agreed. "If I never have to go bowling again in my life, I'll be thrilled."

"I'd die before going back to that miniature golf course," Jessica added. She put her hand to her temple. "I'm even sick of the mall! The new fall fashions won't be coming in for another month."

"If we could only take a vacation," Elizabeth murmured.

Jessica sat up. "Well, the least we can do is get a gorgeous tan."

"I think I'll just work on my story," Elizabeth said, tapping her notebook.

"Fine. But when I come back from the pool, you better show me something brilliant," Jessica told her, as she headed down the stairs for the backyard.

Elizabeth looked at the blank sheet of notebook paper in front of her. Summer would seem worthwhile if she could only write a story. A mystery story. Elizabeth wanted to write something so spectacular that critics would compare her to Amanda Howard. She imagined that her book would become an instant best-seller, making her the most famous person—let alone middle-schooler—ever to have lived in Sweet Valley. She would travel the country speaking to young aspiring novelists and would receive fan mail every day. She would put out a new book every year and teach classes to college students on the side. Amanda Howard would certainly be flattered to learn that Elizabeth Wakefield had been inspired by her.

Elizabeth glanced up at the titles on her shelf. *The Secret Treasure of Tabitha, The Ticking Clock,* and *Victoria's Nightmare* had been three of her favorites. *So what should I call my story?* Elizabeth wondered. That was the right place to start. After all, a wonderful title was often the reason she chose a book.

Elizabeth strummed her fingers. She scribbled the word *Title,* but nothing came to mind. She got up and paced, but she still couldn't think of anything. *Of course,* she realized. *How can I think of a title if I don't know what my mystery is about?* First she had to pick the topic. Elizabeth sat back down at her desk, reenergized, and tore off the top sheet of the pad.

Elizabeth wrote *Topic* in block letters on the top of the sheet. She rolled the pencil along the edge of the paper, thinking. *I wonder how Amanda Howard does it,* Elizabeth mused. There were so many choices to make, she hardly knew where to begin. Should her heroine be a young girl, a college student, or an adult? Should her setting be Sweet Valley, or should she make up a fantasy world where only the strangest things happened? Should her story involve a murder, a robbery, a ghost, or a buried treasure? There were so many elements to writing a mystery, Elizabeth felt overwhelmed. *I guess I never realized how tough it would be,* she thought with frustration.

She wanted to write a book more than anything, but she couldn't get down a single word.

"So let's see it!" Jessica exclaimed as she entered Elizabeth's room, damp from her swim.

"See what?" Elizabeth asked.

Jessica headed straight for the full-length mirror to examine her tan line.

"Your story? You've only been sitting up here for the past three hours. You must have something to show for yourself," Jessica replied.

Elizabeth reluctantly held up the blank pad. "Not exactly."

"Don't tell me you sacrificed getting a golden tan for nothing," Jessica said.

Elizabeth shrugged.

"So what have you been doing? Staring at the wall?" Jessica asked as she tossed her polka-dotted cover-up over her head.

Elizabeth folded her arms over her chest and slumped back in her chair. "Pretty much. Only, writers like to call staring at the wall 'writer's block.' I can't think of anything to write about."

"*You?* Writer's block? But you never have a hard time coming up with ideas for the *Sixers*," Jessica reminded her.

"That's different, Jess. When I write a story for the *Sixers*, it's about something that happened at school or a big event going on in Sweet Valley. It's just reporting. Creative writing is a lot harder. I have to come up with an original story and unique characters and an interesting setting," Elizabeth explained.

Jessica flipped her damp hair and looked back at the books lining the shelf. "Well, Amanda Howard obviously comes up with stuff all the time."

Elizabeth nodded. "I read an article about Amanda Howard that said when she gets writer's block, she goes to her cabin in Northern California. Maybe if I had somewhere peaceful to go I'd have a breakthrough." She sighed as she imagined herself over an antique typewriter with a view of a clear blue lake. "Somehow my bedroom isn't exactly inspiring."

"Hey, maybe I can help," Jessica suggested.

Elizabeth looked at her sister skeptically. "No offense, Jess, but what do you know about writing a book? The only thing you ever read are teen magazines."

Jessica tossed her hair. "Even so, Lizzie, as an actress, I have a natural flair for drama."

Elizabeth folded her arms. "OK, let's hear it. What's your idea?"

Jessica frowned in concentration. "Why don't you write a story about a guy who sees a girl passing by on the Venice canals. It's love at first sight, and after a whirlwind romance, they decide to get married. Only then does he find out that she's really a princess, who was sick of men chasing her for her money. They live happily ever after in the castle, and all the housekeepers and cooks and butlers and staff who work for them fall in love, too."

Elizabeth giggled. "You just described the Johnny Buck movie we saw last week."

"Oh, yeah. I knew it sounded good." Jessica smiled.

"And anyway, that movie was a love story. I'm writing a mystery. There has to be suspense and fear and a brilliant twist at the end."

Jessica bit her lip pensively. "I'm onto something." She stood up and paced around the room. "Write this down, Elizabeth." Jessica cleared her throat. "Once upon a time."

"Once upon a time?" Elizabeth repeated. "That's how fairy tales begin. I have to start with something that evokes a darker mood."

"Fine. Then I have a better beginning." Jessica cleared her throat again. "It was a dark and stormy night," she dictated in a brooding voice.

Elizabeth copied the words onto her pad. "Go on. That's good."

"It was a dark and stormy night," Jessica repeated, then stopped in her tracks. "And, well, I don't know. You're the writer. You figure it out. I have to get the chlorine out of my hair." She headed off to the bathroom.

Elizabeth groaned as she put her pad back in the drawer. One thing was certain. If Elizabeth Wakefield was ever going to become a famous mystery writer, it wasn't going to be with the help of her sister.

Two

"Tuna casserole." Jessica wrinkled her nose as she plopped into her seat. It was dinnertime, and the Wakefields were all sitting around the kitchen table.

"Looks delicious," Mr. Wakefield said, taking a hearty serving.

"Do you realize that as we eat this, Lila is probably dining on caviar with a gorgeous guy at a long table with candelabras somewhere in Switzerland?" Jessica took an unenthusiastic scoop and passed the serving bowl to Steven, her fourteen-year-old brother.

"Do you even know what caviar is?" Steven teased, taking an enormous serving of casserole.

"Fish eggs," Jessica said proudly. "And it's served in an elegant silver dish with a tiny little knife. It's eaten on a plain, thin cracker." At least that was how Lila had described it to her.

"But if you knew what it tasted like, I don't think you'd be jealous of Lila anymore." Steven passed the casserole on to Elizabeth.

"As if you knew anything about fine food," Jessica retorted.

"I'm an encyclopedia on the best food on earth. Burgers, fries, shakes, you name it," Steven said.

Steven had found a summer job selling food at a concession stand by the beach. The menu consisted of nothing but burgers, fries, hot dogs, cotton candy, and shakes. Steven had bragged to Jessica that during his lunch break he was allowed to eat whatever he wanted for free. He had already told her that today's meal had included two cheeseburgers, a hot dog, and a shake in each flavor.

"You have the absolute worst taste in the world, Steven," Jessica continued, as Steven buttered a roll. "You're a junk-food junkie."

"Elizabeth, you haven't touched your food," Mrs. Wakefield said, interrupting, as she looked over at Elizabeth's plate.

"I'm not too hungry, Mom. Sorry," she said glumly, pushing her food around with a fork.

"She's suffering from a terrible illness called writer's block," Jessica teased. "I hope it's not contagious."

"It's not funny, Jess. I want to write a book more

than anything in the world, but I just can't seem to get started. I wish there was someone who could help me." Elizabeth shook her head in frustration. "I never knew it was going to be so hard."

"Wait a second, Elizabeth," Steven cut in. "You're planning to write a book? Don't you think that's just a little ambitious of you? I mean, you're only twelve years old."

"For your information, Elizabeth can do anything she sets her mind to," Jessica informed him.

"She certainly can," Mrs. Wakefield agreed, smiling.

"Besides, there's nothing else to do this summer. I might as well accomplish something," Elizabeth added.

"Yeah." Jessica sighed. "This summer is really a dud."

"Speak for yourselves," Steven taunted. "Too bad you guys are too young to get a great job like mine."

Jessica bristled. She couldn't stand it when Steven used the word *young* to describe her. "Trust me, Steven. When I'm old enough to get a job, it won't be at some greasy burger pit. I'll get a job working at a boutique in the mall. I'll get a discount on all the gorgeous clothes."

"Sounds like you'll never have anything left in your paycheck," Mr. Wakefield remarked.

"But I'll be the best-dressed girl at school,"

Jessica responded. "Even better than Lila."

"I'd love to get a job at the bookstore," Elizabeth mused. "I'd get to see all the new titles and recommend my favorites to the customers."

"But that doesn't exactly help you guys for now," Steven reminded them, gloating. "You're stuck at home every day, while I get to hang out on the beach and serve chocolate milk shakes to girls in bikinis." He raised his eyebrows mischievously.

Jessica rolled her eyes. She didn't understand how any girl could fall for her obnoxious brother.

"It wouldn't be so unbearable if all our friends weren't busy doing other things this summer." Elizabeth sighed. "Maybe I can sign up for the second session of summer school with Amy."

Jessica looked alarmed. "No way, Elizabeth. You'll leave me with no one to hang out with at all. Then this summer would be even worse." She pushed her plate away.

"Maybe this is a good time to tell them," Mr. Wakefield said, smiling at Mrs. Wakefield.

"Tell us what?" Steven asked.

"Actually, Steven, it only involves the girls," Mrs. Wakefield explained.

"Ha!" Jessica exclaimed, smiling at her brother with satisfaction.

Elizabeth perked up in her seat. "What is it? What involves only us?"

"I'll be right back to tell you all about it." Mr. Wakefield got up from the dinner table and disappeared into his study.

"What is it, Mom?" Jessica asked impatiently.

"Well, your father and I have a surprise," Mrs. Wakefield said mysteriously.

"Tell us, tell us, tell us!" Jessica pleaded. She never liked to wait for exciting news.

"It was your father's idea, so let's wait for him to tell you," Mrs. Wakefield said, smiling.

Finally, Mr. Wakefield returned, holding a stack of colorful brochures. Without saying a word, he passed a pamphlet to each of his daughters. On the cover, big green letters above a photograph of a clear blue lake read CAMP FARAWAY.

"Summer camp!" Elizabeth and Jessica exclaimed in unison.

"We've spoken to the Camp Director, and she says there's still time to enroll," Mrs. Wakefield told them. "If you girls agree, we'll enroll you for a two-week session."

"With Steven working and Mom putting in extra hours at the firm, we thought it was only fair for you two to keep busy, too," Mr. Wakefield added.

"I can't believe it," Jessica said, gazing at the back of the brochure. "I've always dreamed about going away to camp. I've never seen such a gorgeous lake. And look, Lizzie—this cabin's totally adorable." Jessica held up a picture of a brown log cabin with quaint red curtains and wooden bunk beds.

Elizabeth looked up with the biggest smile she had cracked all day. "Writing workshops! This is perfect—I'll get the change of atmosphere and the help I need to write my mystery novel."

Suddenly, Jessica felt a pang of alarm. "Wait a minute—this isn't a summer school that's disguised as camp, is it?" she asked her parents.

"Not at all," Mr. Wakefield assured Jessica. "I think there are a few activities you'll be interested in."

"Like what?" Jessica wanted to know.

Mrs. Wakefield's eyes were twinkling. "How about two weeks of dance classes and acting lessons?"

"Really?" Jessica said excitedly.

Elizabeth flipped through the brochure. "There's jazz, ballet, tap, and modern dance, and they put on a play at the end of the camp session."

"Maybe I'll get the lead!" Jessica said hopefully.

Mr. Wakefield grinned. "We figured that Camp Faraway would be suited for you both. There's really something for everyone—swimming, horseback riding, arts and crafts, you name it."

"This is too incredible!" Jessica exclaimed. "Wait till Lila hears—I'd take acting classes and horseback riding over a few plain crackers with caviar any day."

"Who wouldn't?" Elizabeth agreed, as she and Jessica high-fived across the table. Then Elizabeth got up and hugged each of her parents warmly. "Thank you, Mom. Thanks, Dad. This is the best surprise in the world."

"Oh, thank you, thank you, thank you," Jessica added, also standing up to hug her parents. "We're going to have the best two weeks of our lives."

"Well, it sounds pretty boring to me," Steven commented as he helped himself to his third serving of casserole.

"You're just jealous, Steven Wakefield," Jessica retorted. "Too bad you're stuck all summer getting a face full of zits from the french fryer."

"I don't think Steven would fit in anyway. It's a girls' camp," Mr. Wakefield told them.

"And it'll sure be a drag at the end of the summer when I have enough money for a new bike and a bunch of CDs," Steven said sarcastically. "And don't even think about borrowing any of them, Jessica—including *Johnny Buck Live*."

"Even if camp stinks, it will be a vacation getting away from you." Jessica giggled.

"Believe me, the vacation will be mine." Steven turned to his parents. "So when do my evil twin sisters get shipped off?"

Mr. Wakefield served himself some salad. "Day after tomorrow," he said.

"Day after tomorrow?" Jessica repeated. "How will we be ready in time?"

Elizabeth shrugged. "What's to get ready? All

we really need for camp are shorts, a few T-shirts, and bathing suits."

"And Steven already has some camping equipment you can take," Mrs. Wakefield added. "You're just about all set."

"No way, Mom," Jessica said incredulously. "For starters, I'll need to get those cute little travel bottles of shampoo and conditioner." She began ticking off the items on her fingers. "I'll need insect repellent and suntan lotion. I'll definitely need a new swimsuit and a leotard for dance class. I'm thinking red. I'll have to stock up on film so I can take pictures to show the Unicorns. I'll need a new outfit to wear on the first day of camp so I'll make a strong impression. And how on earth will I ever decide what clothes to pack?"

"Why don't you just take your entire wardrobe?" Elizabeth teased. "Didn't you tell me that Lila managed to take everything she owned to Europe?"

"That's a great idea, Lizzie," Jessica said, her eyes lighting up. "Of course, I'll need some new luggage."

Elizabeth laughed. "I was joking."

But Jessica had already made up her mind: she was going to be the best-dressed girl at Camp Faraway.

Three

$\Diamond$

"You don't have to take every single mystery book you own, you know," Jessica pointed out, as she watched Elizabeth neatly transferring the library on her shelf to the bottom of her trunk. The twins were leaving for camp the next day, and Jessica was taking a break from the impossible task of packing.

"But I need them for inspiration," Elizabeth told her. She frowned at her trunk. "I just hope they all fit."

Jessica nodded knowingly. "I can relate. How am I supposed to cram everything I own in that thing?"

Mrs. Wakefield had taken Elizabeth and Jessica to the mall first thing that morning. Jessica stocked up on all the necessities she had mentioned the night before. At the luggage store, Jessica and Elizabeth were each allowed to pick out their very own trunk. Elizabeth selected a sturdy black one, while Jessica chose a purple trunk with lavender trim. She thought it had her name written all over it.

"I don't get it. I mean, the trunk looked so huge in the store, but now that I've started to pack, it seems teeny," Jessica said glumly. "It's like it shrank in the car or something."

Elizabeth laughed. "When I'm through here I'll help you get rid of some stuff. OK?"

Jessica peeked into Elizabeth's open closet, and something caught her eye. "Hey, are you planning to take those pink walking shorts with the matching top? I think they'd be totally perfect for me."

"Jess," her sister scolded, "the idea is to weed things out from your trunk, not add to it!"

"Yikes!" Elizabeth exclaimed, as she stepped into Jessica's room.

Elizabeth carefully looked around. Nothing remained in the closet but a few wire hangers. Clothes flowed out of the trunk to the floor, and the bed was covered with shoes, tapes, magazines, and a set of hot rollers.

"I almost forgot!" Jessica jumped up on a chair and began removing the thumbtacks from her favorite Johnny Buck poster. "Do you think I can somehow fit this in without putting too many creases in Johnny's face?"

Elizabeth stared at all of Jessica's junk in disbelief. "I don't think it's scientifically possible to fit even half of this stuff in that trunk."

"Well, I can't stand the thought of not looking at Johnny Buck for two entire weeks," Jessica told her. "You have to help me find a way to get this in, and we have to be very careful not to damage it."

Elizabeth sighed and gingerly approached the trunk. "Good grief, Jessica, why do you need your purple angora sweater? I mean, it's summertime!"

"You never know when the temperature is going to drop," Jessica said defensively. "And it looks so nice with those white jeans."

"If you want me to help you get organized, Jess, you have to be open-minded," Elizabeth insisted.

"OK, OK. So I won't take the sweater." Jessica tossed it in an open drawer without folding it. "And I guess I can take out my wool coat, too," she added, crumpling it up and aiming for the closet.

"Hey!" Elizabeth snapped as she pulled a pair of her own denim shorts from Jessica's mess. "I've been looking for these everywhere."

"Whoops," Jessica said, putting her hand over her mouth. "I guess I forgot to give them back after I borrowed them to wear on the sixth-grade picnic."

"Yeah, and I guess you forgot to give them back when you were packing them in your trunk," Elizabeth said, her eyes narrowing.

"How about if I take them and you can borrow them?" Jessica suggested dismissively. "You don't have any more room left in your trunk after packing all those mysteries."

"OK, fine," Elizabeth agreed, sighing. "But *this* is a definite waste of space." She removed a red taffeta dress from the pile. "I can pretty much guarantee we won't be going to any formal dances."

"Oh, all *right*," Jessica agreed reluctantly, as her sister hung the dress in the closet.

Elizabeth spent the next half hour putting away various items of Jessica's clothes.

"Just don't remove too much stuff," Jessica warned her. "I need to have options—you never know what's going to come up."

"Don't worry—you could change three times a day and still never have to wear the same thing twice," Elizabeth pointed out. "Anyway, I think we'll be able to close this thing now." She stared at the bulging trunk.

"You sit, I'll lock," Jessica suggested.

Elizabeth dutifully took a seat on top of the trunk. She weighted it down just enough for Jessica to shut the locks.

Elizabeth grinned. "I guess this means we're ready to leave first thing in the morning."

The twins locked eyes. "Camp Faraway, here we come!" they cheered in unison.

*   *   *

"What's in here, Elizabeth, your entire library?" Steven teased as he helped Mr. Wakefield carry her trunk to the station wagon.

Elizabeth grinned sheepishly. "Actually, yes."

"Figures," Steven muttered.

Jessica felt her heart leap with excitement as she watched Steven and her father cart out her own trunk. "Hey, careful!" she warned, as they nearly dropped it on the brick driveway. "My prized possessions are inside."

"It feels like *all* of your possessions are inside," Steven murmured, panting.

Once the trunk was carefully secured on the roof, Jessica eagerly joined Elizabeth in the backseat, ready for the one-hour trip to the bus depot. From the depot, a bus would take all the campers on a four-hour journey to Camp Faraway.

"I guess we're ready to leave," Mrs. Wakefield said as she got into the car and slipped her sunglasses on.

Mr. Wakefield got into the driver's seat. "All aboard!"

Steven looked at his sisters sitting in the backseat. "I never thought I'd hear myself say this, but have fun."

"Thanks, Steven," Elizabeth responded. "Who knows, maybe we'll actually miss you."

"Speak for yourself," Jessica told her. Then she

turned to her brother. "I'm just kidding, Steven. Have fun at the grease pit."

After everyone had buckled up, Mr. Wakefield started the car and pulled down the driveway.

Jessica let out a satisfied sigh as they drove through the neighborhood, passed the bowling alley and miniature golf course, and headed for the freeway. Within a few minutes, she was bored.

"Can you drive any faster, Dad?" Jessica asked anxiously.

"Can't help you out there, Jessica," Mr. Wakefield said patiently.

"Well, when are we going to be there?" she pressed.

"Fifty-five more minutes," Mrs. Wakefield said, taking note of the clock on the dashboard. "It'll fly by."

"We've been driving for an eternity!" Jessica exclaimed. She felt as though she'd been staring at the same boring highway forever.

"Well, only five more minutes to go," Mr. Wakefield assured her. "And then you'll have two whole weeks away."

"Do you think two weeks will be enough time for me to write my novel?" Elizabeth asked eagerly.

"Do you think my acting will improve while we're there?" Jessica asked, without answering her sister's question. "And do you think I should concentrate on jazz or ballet?"

"What do you think the other campers will be like?" Elizabeth wondered.

"There's one good way to find out," Mr. Wakefield said. "Go ahead and meet them." Mr. Wakefield parked the car in a space in front of the terminal.

Jessica peeked in the rearview mirror to make sure her hair hadn't gotten messy during the ride. Satisfied, she hopped out of the car and looked around excitedly. Girls were scattered around saying farewells to their families and stuffing their belongings into the luggage compartment on the side of the bus.

"I guess this is it." Mrs. Wakefield looked at her daughters fondly once the girls had transferred their things to the bus. "Now, look after each other and make sure to write. And brush your teeth three times a day."

Jessica rolled her eyes. "Sheesh, Mom, we know how to take care of ourselves. We're practically teenagers, you know."

"It's true, Mom," Elizabeth added sweetly. "We'll be just fine."

"Make this a memorable summer," Mr. Wakefield said with a wink. "We'll miss the havoc around the house."

*   *   *

"I wonder where all these girls go to school," Elizabeth whispered once she and Jessica were sitting on the bus.

Jessica looked straight ahead with a frown. "How weird. That girl looks like Mandy Miller."

Elizabeth followed Jessica's gaze. The girl she was staring at was coming up the aisle, checking for empty seats. She wasn't necessarily pretty, but she stood out from the other campers. Her shiny waist-length hair was pulled into a ponytail with multicolored ribbons, and she wore a pair of oversized purple overalls with a yellow tank top underneath.

"Jess!" Elizabeth cried happily. "That *is* Mandy Miller."

Mandy was one of the few friends that Elizabeth and Jessica shared. Elizabeth thought she was one of the few Unicorns who were nice and thoughtful.

"Mandy!" the twins yelled simultaneously.

Mandy widened her eyes. "Oh, my gosh! What are you guys doing here?" she asked, as she jumped up and walked along the aisle toward them. "I thought you were spending the whole summer in Sweet Valley."

"So did we," Elizabeth told her. "But we got lucky at the last minute."

Mandy giggled. "Me, too. I was already dying of boredom."

"I can't believe you're here!" Jessica exclaimed.

"I knew this camp was going to be the coolest place on earth."

"Is this seat taken?" asked a tall, pretty girl with brown, wavy hair and big blue eyes. She pointed to the spot next to Mandy.

"Go ahead," Mandy offered. "I'm Mandy Miller. And these are the Wakefields."

"Jessica," Jessica said with a friendly wave.

"And Elizabeth," Elizabeth said with a smile. "We all go to Sweet Valley Middle School together."

"My name's Miranda Page," the girl said confidently. "I'm going to Faraway for the acting program. How about you?"

"Me, too!" Jessica exclaimed. She tossed her hair. "I'm going to be an actress when I grow up."

"I'm psyched to try out for the play," Mandy added. "I hope there's a part for a comic sidekick."

"What about you, Elizabeth?" Miranda asked.

"Actually, I'm more interested in the writing workshops," Elizabeth replied.

Miranda raised her eyebrows. "Writing? At summer camp? Is there such a thing?"

"'My verse alone had all thy gentle grace; And my sick Muse doth give another place.'"

Elizabeth looked up in surprise. The girl in the seat in front of them had turned around to face them. She was African-American and had stunning dark eyes and a soft smile.

"Excuse me?" Elizabeth said shyly.

"Sounds like Shakespeare," Miranda said, looking at the girl quizzically.

"It *is* Shakespeare. I just quoted from one of his sonnets," the girl explained.

Elizabeth smiled. "It's beautiful."

"So do you actually know lots of Shakespeare by heart?" Miranda wanted to know. "I played Lady Macbeth in our school production of the play, and let me tell you, it took forever to memorize all those lines."

"Wow! You starred in *Macbeth*?" Jessica exclaimed.

"'Double, double toil and trouble; Fire burn and cauldron bubble,'" Miranda and the girl in front said in unison. Then they burst into laughter.

"A famous line from the play," Miranda explained, still giggling.

"By the way, I'm Starr Johnson," the girl said.

"I'm Elizabeth Wakefield." Elizabeth introduced the rest of the girls. "So you're a real Shakespeare buff, huh?"

"I guess you could say that," Starr replied modestly. "I totally love writing and reading poetry. How about you? What do you write?"

"I love practically all books, but mysteries are my favorite," Elizabeth told her. "Especially Amanda Howard. I've read every one of her books."

"At least twice," Jessica teased.

"I brought them all along, so let me know if you

want to borrow one," Elizabeth offered. "*The Ticking Clock* is totally amazing."

Starr shivered. "Thanks, but I get spooked out kind of easily. Don't those books give you nightmares?"

Elizabeth smiled. "They can be pretty scary, but that's one thing I love about them. I'm planning to write a mystery novel myself."

"'Like as the waves make towards the pebbled shore; Each changing place with that which goes before,'" Starr quoted. "I like journalism, too," she added without pausing. "I write on the school paper back at home."

"Hey, so do I!" Elizabeth looked at Starr appreciatively. She seemed kooky and a lot of fun. *Looks like both Jess and I found people we have stuff in common with. Camp is turning out to be a blast already!*

Four

I can't believe we're here, Elizabeth thought as she stepped off the bus and waited on line to receive her cabin assignment. Elizabeth took a deep breath. The dense trees filled the air with a clean, fresh, piney scent she had never smelled before. The atmosphere seemed almost electric. *If there were ever a perfect surrounding for me to write my masterpiece, I've just found it.*

"That is the cutest sweatshirt I've ever seen," Jessica told a counselor who had approached the twins on line.

The counselor smiled. "The camp store has Camp Faraway sweatshirts in lots of different colors. But for now, I think you might want to get settled. I just need your names."

"Elizabeth and Jessica Wakefield," Elizabeth told her promptly.

Jessica and Elizabeth each received a card that told them to report to Cabin Windelwisp.

"Your trunks will be delivered up there shortly," the counselor added, and she pointed them on their way.

"Look at how adorable it is!" Jessica exclaimed, as they approached the stone path to the log cabin. "It's even better than it looked in that brochure."

"It's picture perfect," Elizabeth agreed, noticing the tiny yellow wildflowers that dotted the cabin's border.

As the twins stepped inside the cabin, Elizabeth felt another surge of excitement. Four sets of wooden bunk beds lined the walls. In the center of the room, a colorful hand-woven rug covered the floor. On the far side of the cabin, a big window offered a spectacular view of Emerald Lake.

"Hey, you guys!" Miranda was sitting on one of the beds, clothes spilling out of her trunk. "Looks like we're cabin mates."

"Cool!" Jessica replied.

"Listen, Jessica, do you want to share a bunk?" Miranda said eagerly.

The twins looked at each other for a moment. "Go for it, Jess," Elizabeth told her. She *had* planned on sharing a bunk with her sister, but she realized it might be fun to share something with a new friend.

Jessica turned back to Miranda. "If I can be on top."

"Then it's all set," Miranda replied.

"Hey, strangers. Long time no see."

Elizabeth turned to see Starr walk into the cabin.

"Hi, Starr!" Elizabeth said. "I'm looking for a bunk mate. What do you say?"

"'Misery acquaints a man with strange bedfellows,'" Starr replied.

Elizabeth raised her eyebrows. "What's that?"

"Oh, it's a famous line from *The Tempest*," Starr explained. "It means that similar interests bring people together. In other words, consider me your bunk mate."

"I hope you're organized, Starr," Jessica warned, "because Elizabeth is a neat freak times ten."

Elizabeth glanced at her sister. "I hope you can tolerate a pigsty, Miranda," she said, "because I can guarantee that within an hour it will look like a tornado has hit over there!"

"A few more campers should be coming in, but for now let me see if I can get you guys straight so far." Once they'd spent a little while getting settled, the Windelwisp campers had gathered around their counselor, Holly Stanton. Holly had long tan legs and short, dark-brown hair. She wore worn suede hiking boots and a red bandanna tied loosely around her neck. She looked down at a printout of names. "Miranda?"

"Miranda Page," Miranda clarified, flipping her wavy hair over her shoulders.

"Starr?" Holly continued.

Starr nodded. "You got it."

Holly squinted her eyes and looked from Elizabeth to Jessica.

"Jessica?" she said to Elizabeth.

Jessica shook her head. "If you want to know how to tell me and Elizabeth apart, I'll give you some simple advice. It's . . ."

". . . truly and utterly unbelievably impossible," Mandy broke in as she walked into the cabin. "I've known Jessica and Elizabeth forever, and I even make a mistake every once in a while."

The twins, Starr, and Miranda greeted Mandy enthusiastically.

Danielle Bruiz, Nicole Goldner, and Melinda Henderson came in shortly after, and rounded out the eight-girl cabin.

"You guys are in for quite an awesome time together," Holly told them. "I should know—I was a camper here for five years. In the fall I'll be a senior at University High in San Diego, so this is my last year here."

"So I guess we better make it an incredibly excellent farewell to Faraway for you," Mandy mused.

Holly smiled. "Sounds good by me. Soon as you're ready, we'll all walk over to the welcome bonfire."

Jessica looked down at her wrinkled lavender blouse distastefully. "As soon as I change."

"Really," Miranda agreed, moving toward her trunk. "What do you wear to a bonfire?"

"Something casual yet stylish," Jessica told her, as she dug into her wardrobe. "By the way, Holly, where's the full-length mirror?"

Holly laughed. "This is camp, Jessica. You're supposed to rough it."

"The words *rough it* aren't in Jessica's vocabulary," Elizabeth warned.

"Just give her time," Holly said, tugging at her cutoff shorts.

"I guess we'll have to deal with the mirror above the bathroom sink," Miranda said.

Jessica sighed. "It's better than nothing."

By the time the Windelwisp campers started walking to the central campsite, the sun had begun to set. Elizabeth looked out at the scenery in awe. It was the most beautiful place she had been in her entire life.

"There are a few rules I should go over with you guys," Holly explained along the way.

"Rules?" Jessica repeated grimly. "You're kidding."

"They're not too harsh, guys, but listen up," Holly said. "First of all, lights out means lights out."

Jessica grunted. "Yeah, right," she whispered to Miranda.

"Second, you may never leave the campgrounds unless you're accompanied by a counselor. And finally, the most important rule regards Emerald Lake. No swimming or canoeing after dark. Ever."

"Who would even want to?" Starr asked, shuddering.

"Plus, you may never go out on the lake alone," Holly continued. She looked back at the group. "Questions? Comments? Complaints?"

"They sound fair to me," Elizabeth said.

"I guess they're not *too* bad," Jessica admitted.

"And as long as everyone abides by them, we won't have any problems," Holly concluded. "And speaking of Emerald Lake, everything is built around it. That's the mess hall, those are the stables"—she gestured with her hand—"and here's the picnic area."

Hot dogs and hamburgers were cooking over a big barbecue pit, and campers were already waiting on line.

"Steven would be in seventh heaven," Elizabeth said, as she took a hamburger and a handful of chips.

"Don't mention that name, Lizzie," Jessica pleaded. "We escaped from him, remember?"

"If you're talking brothers, I can relate," Miranda complained. "I have a little brother who likes to hide my portable phone and put toothpaste on the toilet seat."

"'Lord, what fools these mortals be!'" Starr exclaimed.

Elizabeth giggled. "Which, of course, comes from—?"

"*A Midsummer Night's Dream*," Starr said. "I have a hyperactive brother, too."

"I like that one," Jessica admitted, as they found a spot at the end of a large picnic bench. "Next time Steven tries to torture me, I'll tell him that."

"Oh, that'll stop him in his tracks," Elizabeth joked.

"Well, maybe he's a fool, but their brother is seriously gorgeous," Mandy told Starr and Miranda.

"Gross!" Jessica gasped. "You can't possibly mean that."

"Are you sure we're talking about the same person?" Elizabeth asked.

Mandy smiled mischievously. "You guys just can't see it."

Elizabeth rolled her eyes. "I'm getting some more chips," Elizabeth said. "Come on, Jess."

"I hope you've all had time to begin getting acquainted," said a woman who approached the campfire. Night had fallen, and the campers were huddling around the fire to make s'mores. The woman's gray hair was tied in a long braid, and her jeans were rolled up at the bottom, revealing red-and-white striped socks worn with blue sneakers. "Welcome to Camp Faraway. I'm Gunnie Mapleman."

Elizabeth remembered reading in the brochure that Gunnie Mapleman was the owner of the camp. Instantly, she could tell that there was something special about her. Elizabeth hoped that she'd have a chance to get to know her during the session.

"Having traveled the world many a time," Gunnie said in an elegant voice, "I've always found that I enjoy what I see more when I know a bit of the history behind it."

"History," Jessica gasped quietly. "Who cares?"

"Not me, that's for sure," Miranda whispered. "If I had wanted a history lesson, I could have stayed behind and gone to that crummy summer school in Los Angeles."

"You might roll your eyes at the idea of history," Gunnie said knowingly, "but Camp Faraway has a special history of its own. Some things I will share with you tonight, others you will learn for yourselves as you spend time here." Gunnie raised her eyebrows. "Camp Faraway is a place of many legends. There's more here than meets the eye."

Elizabeth gazed at Gunnie, mesmerized.

"Many famous people have spent time on the grounds," Gunnie continued.

Jessica nudged Miranda. "Famous people?"

"Maybe the people in the acting program went on to Hollywood or Broadway or something," Miranda said hopefully.

"Perhaps the most famous person to be associated

with the site is the notorious Roland Barge," Gunnie went on.

Miranda wrinkled her nose. "Who?"

"Roland Barge," Elizabeth repeated in a whisper. "He's a famous novelist from the 1940s."

"He was one of the greatest mystery writers of all time," Gunnie went on. "His books were bestsellers in his time and are now considered classics. They're all available in the Faraway Library, which is just behind us." She pointed toward a little redwood building.

"There's no way I'm spending my summer in a library," Jessica whispered.

"As you look around, you also see Emerald Lake, the forest, and all the wildflowers," Gunnie continued. "The mess hall is that way, the dance studio is through there, and all the cabins are scattered throughout." She paused for a moment as she scanned the audience before her. "But what you don't see yet is my very favorite part of the land. The many miles of caves that extend underground."

Starr frowned. "It didn't say anything in the brochure about caves." She huddled closer to Elizabeth.

Gunnie's eyes took on an eerie glow from the firelight. "If you think that sounds spooky, some say that many years ago, murders were committed on this property," she confided in a soft, foreboding tone.

Starr gasped.

"Murders?" Jessica repeated, her voice shaking slightly.

Elizabeth felt a little flicker of alarm.

Gunnie looked out at her captive audience. "Perhaps that's just a bit of folklore, passed down through the generations. There's no documented evidence of any such crimes."

As Gunnie paused, loons on Emerald Lake cried out to each other in the distance.

A few campers shrieked aloud at the eerie sound. Starr grasped on to Elizabeth tightly. Even Gunnie looked a bit startled by the noise.

"There's no reason to be so alarmed," Gunnie said, collecting herself. "As I said, nothing has ever been proved."

But Elizabeth's eyes had grown wide with intrigue. Maybe she'd write a mystery about something that had actually taken place on the site. And maybe Gunnie knew more about the supposed murders than she had let on.

Five

"What is *that*?" Jessica moaned the next morning.

The sound of a bugle blasted through the loud-speaker in Windelwisp.

Jessica put her pillow over her head. *This is worse than my alarm clock.*

"Is this boot camp or summer camp?" Miranda grumbled from the lower bunk. "Can somebody please turn that down?"

After the music faded out, Gunnie's chipper voice came through the speaker loud and clear. "Good morning, campers. It's seven o'clock, and it's time to get up, up, up and start the day with a smile. Breakfast will be served in ten minutes in the main dining hall. Regular schedules will begin tomorrow. Today you'll get a chance to become acquainted with all the camp facilities. Remember to wear hiking boots and bring your canteens, because we'll be splitting up in groups and going on cave expeditions throughout the day. Cheerio!"

"This can't be happening," Jessica said with a yawn. "I've slept in since school got out. I think I even forgot how to set my alarm clock." She hung over the top bunk and peeked down at Miranda.

"This is against my principles," Miranda replied, slowly opening her eyes. "I'll look like an absolute wreck today."

"Ditto," Jessica replied. "I thought this was a vacation."

"What are you supposed to wear on a cave expedition, anyway?" Miranda asked in a groggy voice.

Jessica perked up slightly. Fashion talk had a strange way of doing that to her. "Something rugged, yet sporty." She sat up in bed and noticed that Elizabeth and Starr were already getting dressed for the day. "Why do they look so *awake*?"

"Probably because they didn't stay up after lights out gossiping about boys," Miranda suggested.

"All right, guys," Holly called to Jessica and Miranda. "Let's get a move on."

"Just five more minutes?" Jessica moaned. "Please, Holly?"

Holly folded her arms. "OK," she agreed after a pause. "Just five."

*   *   *

It was almost a half hour later when Jessica and Miranda sauntered into the cafeteria for breakfast, decked out in walking shorts and white sneakers. Elizabeth smiled. *A pretty long five minutes,* she said to herself. But before she could tease them, Holly announced that the cave expedition would start in a few minutes, and everyone should meet by the wooden fence. Elizabeth, Starr, and Mandy had already fueled up on bacon and pancakes, and they dashed outside together.

"I'll be leading the cave expedition," Holly told them. "We'll be joined by the girls from Cabin Snapdragon—and here they are now."

As the girls from Snapdragon gathered around, Holly suggested that everyone take a few minutes to make introductions before they set out to go. Elizabeth met a nice girl from San Francisco named Tracy, and her best friend Christy.

"I'm Priscilla Westover," said a girl with blond, permed hair and a thick Southern accent. "Mommy and Daddy would never have sent me to Camp Faraway if they'd known I was going to be sent on a dangerous cave expedition. What if something happens to me?"

"I'm sure it's perfectly safe," Elizabeth said in her most rational tone of voice. "I doubt that Holly would risk our lives just for the sake of showing us a cave."

"Well, if anything happens to me," Priscilla said, "all I can say is, major lawsuit."

"I won't let anything happen to any of you," Holly assured them. "Now, let's get a move on."

Holly led the group, using a thick tree branch as a walking stick.

"Was that bacon gross, or what?" Priscilla complained. "And that orange juice definitely was not fresh-squeezed."

"It's a mess hall, not a four-star restaurant," Holly told her. "You should probably lower your standards, Priscilla—that way you won't be disappointed again."

"Two weeks of that stuff and I'll probably just waste away to nothing," Priscilla went on. "And it'll be impossible to get a good night's sleep on that crummy mattress."

Elizabeth stifled a sigh. She always tried to see the best in people, but Priscilla Westover was already starting to get on her nerves. "I had the best sleep of my life," she said cheerfully, determined not to let Priscilla get her down. "I woke up before Gunnie's announcement and listened to the birds chirp."

But even Elizabeth began to grow tired as the group hiked farther into the forest.

"All right, troops, here we are," Holly said finally. "This is called Hangman's Cave."

Elizabeth slowly peeked through the mouth of the cave. She could see nothing but darkness. Her heart beat with the same anticipation she felt when she started reading a great mystery story.

Priscilla made a face. "I think I'll just wait for you all out here."

"What a priss," Miranda whispered to her friends.

Jessica giggled. "Figures her name would be Priscilla," she whispered back.

"Actually, I think Prissy has a point," Starr contributed. "That doesn't look very inviting."

"The first time I explored the cave, I was nervous myself," Holly said calmly. "It's just fear of the unknown. There are wonderful treasures to see inside."

"Like what?" Priscilla demanded.

"Let's just wait until we get inside," Holly said. "That's the fun of this tour. For those of you who'd like a little background, you should know that the cave is named after Roland Barge's famous novel *Death of a Hangman*."

Elizabeth felt a tremor of fear. As much as she loved mysteries, that book had always sounded too scary to read. Compared with Roland Barge's dark thrillers, Amanda Howard's mysteries were like fairy tales.

"Everybody pick a buddy first. Then we'll go on in," Holly told the group.

Elizabeth turned to her sister. "Buddies?"

Jessica nodded and they hooked arms.

Miranda partnered with Starr, and Mandy was a sport about ending up with Priscilla. When all the other campers had buddied up, Holly passed out a metal flashlight to each team. "Follow me," Holly said, as she ducked her head inside the cave and motioned for the girls to come along. "We'll take a path down to the lowest point of the cave. Some areas of the path will become very narrow, so you'll have to go single file."

The twins ended up at the back of the group, and Elizabeth shuddered with anticipation as they made their way into Hangman's Cave. The air felt damp, and droplets of water rolled down the walls.

"It's like another world," Elizabeth marveled as she began to move her flashlight along the textured surfaces. She inhaled the strange, musty air.

Icicle-shaped deposits of mud hung from the ceiling, and cone-shaped deposits stuck to the floors. The girls looked closely at the strange figures. Elizabeth couldn't resist rubbing her fingers over the gritty surface.

"The formations hanging from the roof of the cave are called stalactites," Holly told the group. "They are created by the evaporation of dripping water full of lime."

"How disgusting," Priscilla complained. "And it smells so moldy down here."

"The cone-shaped stumps you see are called

stalagmites. They are formed from the drip off of the stalactites." Holly shined her flashlight from the stalactites to the stalagmites.

Elizabeth gazed at the strange formations. "The stalagmites look like modern sculptures I've seen in museums."

Priscilla shook her head. "They look like disgusting blobs of mud to me."

Jessica smiled. "I think they look like upside-down ice cream cones."

Suddenly an eerie pattern leaped across the ceiling.

Jessica clutched Elizabeth's sleeve. "What's that?" she said through gritted teeth.

"I think that's Priscilla's shadow," Elizabeth whispered back.

"This way." Holly motioned the girls around a corner.

They continued through the cave, stopping to look at all the crevices and bumps that surrounded them.

"The path becomes narrow here," Holly said. "Make sure you hold on to the railing as you come along. And if you were planning to ask, *Priscilla*, it's very sturdy. It was just installed last year."

As Elizabeth clung to the rail, she found it looked out over a large, dark pool of water. She leaned over and squinted her eyes. It almost looked as though it were bottomless. *But there's no such thing as a bottomless pool*, she told herself.

The chatter of the group gradually faded out, and Elizabeth was aware of Jessica's especially tight clutch on her arm.

Finally the group made it to a flat surface, where they all huddled together as Holly continued her lecture.

"I know it looks bottomless," Holly told them. "No one has ever measured its depths, but I can assure you it ends not too far below."

Elizabeth shined her flashlight in the pool, but there was no sign of a floor. "What makes you so sure?" Elizabeth asked nervously.

"Logic," Holly responded briskly. "Up ahead the cave extends for miles. It's supposed to be like a maze. I've never gone much farther than this point . . ."

"So we're through?" Starr said. "We can get out of here?"

"Yes," Holly answered, "but before we return to civilization, I want to make sure you're all still with me. Let's do a body count."

"Why?" Jessica bit her lip. "Has anyone ever disappeared here?"

"Don't be silly, Jessica," Holly assured her. "I just wouldn't want to make this time the first. I don't think Gunnie—or, for that matter, your parents— would be too pleased if I misplaced one of you."

Holly began counting off the sixteen campers one by one.

"Augggghhhh!" Priscilla hollered.

Elizabeth was so startled, she screamed in response. Jessica and all the others joined in, too.

All the yelling echoed throughout the cave. It seemed hours before the murmurs faded away.

"It's a bat!" Priscilla yelled. "Run for your life!"

A large bat suddenly swooped down out of nowhere. Its wings made a loud flapping sound as it circled above the group.

Jessica was frozen solid. Elizabeth could feel her sister's fingernails digging into her skin.

Priscilla grabbed on to Holly's sweatshirt and tried to hide.

"Everybody calm down," Holly urged. "Bats are harmless. If anything, they're scared of us."

"Oh, my gosh!" Elizabeth couldn't help but gasp as the bat dove down. It got so close that she could see little black hairs covering its body.

"Get me out of here, Holly!" Priscilla wailed. "Now!"

The bat disappeared as quickly as it had appeared, but Priscilla was already frantically pushing the girls away. She tripped over a bump on the ground and grabbed for Elizabeth's arm to avoid falling flat on her face. Elizabeth slipped and fell down with a thump, the wind momentarily knocked out of her.

"Lizzie!" Jessica cried. "Are you all right?" She kneeled at her sister's side.

"I'm OK, Jess," Elizabeth said, trying to catch her breath.

Holly moved toward Elizabeth.

"I'll be OK, Holly. Just give me a second," Elizabeth said, still winded.

"Nice one, Priscilla," Jessica commented. She looked up at Priscilla, who was now standing calmly near the wall of the cave.

"Well, it's not like I did it on purpose or anything," Priscilla retorted.

"Come on, you guys, there's no use fighting over this," Elizabeth said. "I'm—" She broke off when something caught her eye. In a small crevice at the base of the wall, something was glowing.

"You could have sent my sister flying over into that bottomless pool of water," Jessica scolded.

As the others continued to argue, Elizabeth quickly scooted over and reached for the shining object. It was tightly lodged, and she jimmied it around with her pinkie finger.

"Priscilla does have a point about getting out of here as soon as possible," Mandy argued.

"Whose side are you on?" Jessica demanded.

"Obviously, mine!" Priscilla taunted.

Elizabeth continued to jiggle the object. *Almost*, Elizabeth thought, *I've almost got it!*

"That's not what I meant," Mandy protested. "It was just a mistake. There's no side to be on."

"Why don't you just apologize to her, Priscilla, and we can go back to the mess hall for lunch," Holly said diplomatically.

Finally the object slipped out. Elizabeth couldn't believe her eyes. It was a beautiful, ornate antique fountain pen. It was made of a shiny red stone carved so thinly that it was translucent. And from the inside, something was making the pen glow. Elizabeth had never seen anything like it in her entire life. A million questions raced through her mind. *How did this get here? Who does it belong to? Do they know it's missing? How long has it been there?*

Elizabeth quickly slipped the pen into the front pocket of her blue jeans. Instinctively, she thought it wouldn't be a good idea to show the other campers and have everybody make a fuss about it. There was only one other person Elizabeth felt should know about her discovery. Later, in private, she would show it to her twin.

She looked up from the floor of the cave. "One of you guys want to help me up, or are you going to leave me down here all day long?"

Holly reached over, grasped Elizabeth's hand, and pulled her off the damp floor.

"I'm sorry, Elizabeth," Priscilla finally said.

Elizabeth brushed the dirt off her pants.

"Apology accepted," she replied sweetly, though secretly she didn't think Priscilla had anything to apologize for. If it weren't for Priscilla, in fact, Elizabeth would never have discovered the strange glowing pen.

Six

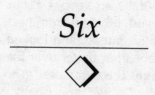

"So what's up, Elizabeth? What's this super-important thing you have to tell me?"

The twins were walking along Emerald Lake on their way back to the cabin. Elizabeth looked out at the lake in a reverie. The sky was clear, and the light from the moon shone down on the water, making it gleam. The wind blew lightly, and little ripples moved across the lake.

Elizabeth sighed contentedly. "It's so beautiful here, I wish I never, ever had to leave."

"You dragged me away from the mess hall to tell me that?" Jessica asked.

Elizabeth giggled. "Not exactly. Actually, I wanted to tell you that I found something today. A pen." She reached her hand into the pocket of her jeans.

"A pen?" Jessica frowned. "Your big news is a pen?"

"It's a special pen, Jess. Look." Elizabeth pulled out the pen and handed it to her sister.

"What could be so special about a dumb old pen?" Jessica said, taking it from her. "It's just a—" She stopped midsentence and looked at the pen in shock. She rubbed her finger over the textured surface and brought the pen close up to examine the intricate detail. "Wow," she finally said. "It's so fancy—I mean, it's almost like a piece of jewelry or something. Where did you find it?"

"In the cave. I noticed it when Priscilla knocked me over," Elizabeth explained.

Jessica looked puzzled. "But it was so dark. How did you see it in there?"

"That's the strangest thing about it, Jess. It was glowing," Elizabeth said. "Like a battery was lighting it up from the inside."

Jessica rolled her eyes. "Come on, Elizabeth. There's no such thing as a glowing pen. Unless it's the glow-in-the-dark kind you buy in a toy store."

Elizabeth looked at her sister seriously. "I know this sounds crazy, but it's almost as if it was lighting itself up for me, so I would notice it and take it out of there."

Jessica raised an eyebrow. "You're right—that's crazy. I think the cave air might have seeped into your brain and turned you into a complete nutcase."

Elizabeth sighed with frustration. "I just have a weird feeling about it."

"What's with you, Elizabeth?" Jessica asked. "Aren't you supposed to be the sensible one—? Whoa!" Suddenly, the pen lit up, and Jessica dropped it.

Elizabeth reached over and picked it up off the ground. "*Now* do you believe me?"

Jessica looked around suspiciously. "This is a trick. Starr is in on this, right?"

"It's not a trick, Jess," Elizabeth said with defiance.

"Really?" Jessica pressed.

"Cross my heart," Elizabeth said.

"Well, I bet Miranda will think this is really pretty. She loves red," Jessica mused.

Elizabeth slid the pen back into her pocket. "No one can see it, Jessica. This is between you and me."

"A secret pen?" Jessica asked. "Oh, come on, Elizabeth. What's the point of hiding it from our friends?"

Elizabeth took a deep breath. "I can't really explain it, but I just have this weird feeling the pen was meant for me. I mean, just as I'm suffering from writer's block, I find this really amazing pen—in a cave, of all places. What are the chances of that?"

Jessica shook her head. "You really are losing it, Elizabeth. You actually think the pen was *meant* for you? What if someone lost it? Then what you're doing is like stealing."

"I have a feeling that it's been there for a really really long time, Jess. I don't think it belongs to anyone at Camp Faraway," Elizabeth explained. "Besides, I just want to borrow it for a little while. Eventually, I'll either put it back where I found it or turn it in to Gunnie. I just want to try using it to write my book."

"Maybe you should write a story about a weird girl who finds a pen and thinks it has magical powers," Jessica suggested.

"Very funny," Elizabeth said, shaking her head.

But Jessica seemed to find it hysterical and couldn't stop laughing.

"Not again," Jessica moaned over the sound of the blasting bugle.

"It's pure torture," Miranda mumbled from the lower bunk.

The second morning started much as the first one had. Gunnie's music came through the loudspeaker, awakening a very chipper Elizabeth and Starr and a very groggy Jessica and Miranda.

Jessica yawned as the bugle music faded out. "And I was in the middle of such a good dream! I think Johnny Buck was just about to propose to me."

"Good morning, campers. It's seven o'clock, and it's time to get up, up, up and start the day with a smile," Gunnie's voice announced. "Today is the first day of full camp schedules. Your cabin counselor will provide you each with a printout of your personal activities. Have fun, and cheerio!"

"Oh, man," Jessica said, pulling herself out from under the covers. "I'm going to need a vacation to recover from my vacation."

"Let's move it, troops," Holly yelled across the room to Jessica and Miranda.

"Five more minutes, Holly? Please," Jessica begged.

"Not today, Jessica," Holly said. "We're on a tight schedule from now on."

Jessica somehow managed to drag herself out of bed and get ready for the day ahead. Once everyone else was dressed and ready to go, Holly handed each of them her own printout.

Jessica took her sheet from Holly. "Let's see," she said. "I have swimming first, then horseback riding. After lunchtime, I spend the afternoon in my dance and acting classes."

"This is great, Jess," Elizabeth said, reading off her own schedule. "We'll be together all morning. In the afternoon I have journalism and pottery class."

" 'There's a divinity that shapes our ends'!" Starr exclaimed, waving her schedule at Elizabeth.

"Let me guess," Elizabeth said, smiling. "You and I are in every period together?"

"Exactly," Starr told her. "You're getting good at this."

Mandy's and Miranda's schedules matched up exactly with Jessica's, and they all high-fived with excitement.

"Check it out." Jessica walked into the theater and looked around in amazmnet.

The stage floor was covered in dark-brown wood, and a regal maroon velvet curtain matched the seat covers in the stalls. Jessica imagined herself making her starring debut and wiggled with excitement.

"It's beautiful," Miranda agreed. "I bet it's just like a theater on Broadway."

About twenty other girls had already come into the room and were seated in the fancy seats. Jessica waved when she noticed her cabin mates Nicole and Danielle.

Gunnie appeared on stage and looked down at the girls chattering in the stalls.

"I wonder what Gunnie's doing here," Jessica said.

"Maybe she's a judge for the play," Mandy guessed. "Maybe she needs to observe the class to see who has talent."

"All right, girls, settle down," Gunnie said in a raised voice.

Jessica, Miranda, and Mandy took their seats in the front row.

"I'll be conducting the acting workshops," Gunnie told the girls with a smile. "It's my favorite part of running camp, and I take this course very seriously."

Jessica felt another wave of excitement. As annoying as it was to hear Gunnie's voice over the loudspeaker so early in the morning, Jessica could tell that the woman would be an excellent acting coach. Her voice and her manner were so elegant.

"I've seen great theater all around the world, and I hold high standards for the Faraway production we'll put on the last day of camp," Gunnie continued. "The play I've selected is a charming farce called *The Royal Switch*."

"*The Royal Switch*?" Miranda looked disappointed.

"Is it a stupid play?" Jessica asked.

"No. It's awesome. It's just that we put on a production of it at my school last year," Miranda said.

"You're kidding," Jessica replied. "Did you have a good part?"

Miranda sighed. "Yeah. I was Penelope. The lead."

Before Jessica could respond, Gunnie continued. "Tryouts will be tomorrow, and I'll pass out the script to each of you at the end of class. I've inserted a list of the scenes you need to be prepared to audition with. You're free to go out for any part you like, but there are some wonderful supporting roles here—I hope not all of you set your hearts on playing Penelope, the lead."

"The lead—how wonderful!" Priscilla exclaimed.

"I wonder if Prissy knows what she's in for," Miranda whispered to Jessica. "It's a really demanding role."

But demanding or not, Jessica already *did* have her heart set on getting the role of Penelope—even if that meant competing against Miranda.

"I'd like to begin today with some improvisational exercises up on stage," Gunnie announced. "It's a good way for me to get a feeling for your movement and style."

"Can I go first?" said a loud Southern voice from the back of the room.

Jessica whipped her head around. Priscilla Westover was eagerly waving her hand to get Gunnie's attention.

"Prissy?" Jessica said under her breath.

"Pretty please?" Priscilla continued.

"Certainly," Gunnie said. "Why don't you come up on stage and tell the group your name. And I'd like you to let us know what your favorite hobbies are. But you have to show us, not tell us."

Priscilla fluffed her blond curls. "You mean like pantomime?" she said on her way up.

Gunnie was leaving the stage to take a seat in the audience. "Exactly."

Priscilla cleared her throat. "For those of you

who don't already know, I'm the one and only Priscilla Westover." Priscilla's accent sounded thicker and more pronounced than ever. "My favorite hobbies are . . ." Priscilla started dancing around the room as if she had a partner on a dance floor.

"Ballroom dancing?" Miranda whispered to Jessica. "Figures."

"I bet she's never even heard of Johnny Buck," Jessica whispered back.

When she was done, Priscilla rushed out to the middle of the stage and curtsied.

"That was very nice, Priscilla," Gunnie said. "Who'd like to go next?"

Jessica raised her hand. "May I?" she asked politely, not wanting to seem overeager.

Gunnie nodded.

Jessica walked to the stage and sat down on a chair. "I'm Jessica Wakefield." She pretended to look in a mirror and put on makeup. She started with blush, then added mascara and eye shadow. She ended by opening a lipstick and smacking her lips together.

Jessica looked out into the crowd before she continued with her next hobby. Gunnie didn't crack a smile. *Well, maybe she's not the wildly applauding type,* Jessica thought, hoping that Gunnie was impressed anyway.

Jessica moved the chair to the other side of the

stage. She pretended she was in a movie theater and watched the screen while nibbling on popcorn. Jessica made laughing and crying faces as she imagined Johnny Buck in one of her favorite movies. She clapped at the end.

"Good job, Jess," Miranda said sincerely. "I loved the way you put on that lipstick."

"Thanks," Jessica told her, a little surprised. Whenever she competed with Lila or the other Unicorns, they never admitted that she'd done a good job. *Is it because Miranda's super confident?*

"I'd like to go next," Miranda announced in her clear, strong voice.

Miranda gracefully proceeded to the stage and showed the girls her demonstration of a tennis match. Jessica held her breath. Miranda was so effective, Jessica could have sworn she saw the tennis ball flying through the air. Her hair shone in the theater lights, and she swung her arms with an easy grace. *She's just like a movie star*, Jessica thought. *A natural.*

As Miranda went on to paint a picture on an easel, Jessica bit her lip. It wasn't that she wasn't happy her friend was so talented, it was that she had to admit she felt a flicker of worry. No doubt about it—Miranda would be tough competition. But Jessica Wakefield wouldn't give up the starring role without a fight.

*   *   *

"The purpose of this class is twofold," Lisa Newman, the writing teacher, told the campers in the workshop. Lisa was thin and tall and had brown, curly hair that rested on her forehead in ringlets. "We'll spend time with both creative writing and journalistic writing."

Elizabeth smiled. She loved both forms of writing, and she couldn't help but think she had some kind of secret advantage. The red pen was so strange and beautiful, she felt sure she'd be able to compose something great with it. She could hardly wait to try it out.

Lisa adjusted her glasses. "At the end of camp, we'll put out a newspaper of our own. I like to consider it a sort of yearbook that captures a bit of Camp Faraway, past and present. Now, for starters, I'd like somebody to do a feature article on Holly Stanton," Lisa said. "It's her last summer at camp, and it would be nice to get an interview of her reflecting on her experiences here."

Starr, who was sitting next to Elizabeth, raised her hand. "Holly's my counselor in Windelwisp. I'll get you an up-close and personal account if you give me the assignment."

"Sounds great," Lisa responded.

Tracy volunteered to do an article on the drama group and a profile of the preparation for their play.

"I also thought it would be interesting to include

a feature article about the great mystery writer Roland Barge," Lisa said.

"I'll do it!" Elizabeth called out eagerly, raising her hand up high. "I would really love to write the article."

"Then it's settled, Elizabeth," Lisa said with a smile.

But Elizabeth's smile was wider. *This is perfect,* she thought. Studying the great author would give her inspiration for her own novel. *And what a great opportunity to use the pen!*

Seven

"After dinner we're supposed to go to the main lodge," Holly said, as everyone finished up dinner in the mess hall.

Elizabeth slumped in her seat. Normally, she would have loved participating in camp activities and hanging out with fellow campers. But she was eager to start work on her article, and she really wanted privacy so that she could use the beautiful red pen.

"There's going to be a bingo game," Holly continued. "Now, don't make a face, you guys. It'll be really fun, and there'll be some great prizes."

"Prizes?" Jessica said, suddenly enticed.

"And one of the counselors is going to teach all the camp songs on her guitar," Holly told them.

"Cool. I love camp songs almost as much as Shakespeare," Starr mused.

"You guys can all hang out there until lights out," Holly said. "There'll be refreshments and a fire going all night. As soon as you've all finished eating, we can head over together."

"Let's go now so we can get the best seats in the house," Miranda said, scooping up the last bite of her dessert.

"Hold on," Elizabeth said suddenly. Before she realized what she was doing, she put her hand to her forehead. "I don't know if I should go—I feel awful. Just awful."

"What's wrong with you?" Jessica asked, twirling a strand of hair around her finger.

Holly looked concerned. "Is it something you ate?"

"Headache. A pretty terrible one," Elizabeth said, faking as she held her fingers to her temples.

"You do look a little pale," Miranda said, leaning up close to Elizabeth.

"It's my throat, too." Elizabeth coughed to add drama.

"If you're feeling under the weather, you're probably better off relaxing in the cabin," Holly suggested. "It's not like you'll be missing one of the highlights of camp, like the lakeside serenade later in the week."

Elizabeth nodded. "That's a good idea. I wouldn't want to push it and feel sick all day tomorrow."

"'Time doth transfix the flourish set on youth; Feeds on the rarities of nature's truth.'" Starr patted

Elizabeth's shoulder. "I hope you feel better, Elizabeth. I'll teach you all the songs if you want."

"We'll be back in at Windelwisp in a few hours," Holly told her. "Are you sure you'll be OK?"

"Oh, I'll be fine," Elizabeth assured her. "I just need a little quiet time."

Elizabeth cuddled up on the top bunk and looked out the window onto Emerald Lake. She could hardly believe how she'd acted in the mess hall—it was totally unlike her to pretend to be sick to get out of doing anything. That was Jessica's department. But somehow she felt as though she *had* to find time alone—it was almost as though the pen were calling to her.

She took out the Roland Barge biography she'd checked out of the library and a blank pad of paper. Then she carefully pulled the pen out from under the mattress where she had hidden it.

Where do I begin the article? Elizabeth wondered. *With Roland Barge's childhood? A discussion of his earliest novels? Or his time spent on what would become the Faraway premises? What would the readers most like to know?* she asked herself. *What would pull them into the article and hold their interest?*

Elizabeth tapped the pen, thinking.

Suddenly, she felt something pulling her hand toward the paper. She started furiously scribbling as words began coming to her. The words flew from her hand in a mystical way, almost as if they were writing themselves. After she completed a page, her hand ached from the intensity and speed of her writing.

Elizabeth exhaled, put down the pen, and looked at the pad. *What's going on?* The handwriting didn't even look like hers. Elizabeth liked to print in neat block letters, but the sheet was covered with beautiful slanted cursive. And even stranger, what she'd written seemed to have nothing to do with Roland Barge. Elizabeth had somehow begun a story about a girl named Amelia Champlain. *Who's Amelia Champlain, and how'd I end up writing about her?* Elizabeth wondered, as goose bumps formed on her arms.

Suddenly, something pulled her hand back to the paper, and she continued the story, her hand gliding smoothly and effortlessly across the page.

This is crazy, she said to herself when her hand stopped again. *Who ever heard of a story taking shape so quickly?* On the other hand, maybe it was part of the creative process. She had been thinking so long and hard about what her mystery would be about that maybe it was just bursting to come out. *This probably happens to Amanda Howard all the time,* Elizabeth rationalized.

Elizabeth settled back on the pillow and began to read. *So much for my mystery,* Elizabeth thought, frowning. Instead, she had begun to write a love story that took place at the site of Camp Faraway over seventy years before. In place of the mess hall and the theater arts building was a palatial estate called O'Neil Manor. The O'Neils had come over from Ireland in the early 1900s and had chosen the site for their summer home because of the magnificence of Emerald Lake. But the story didn't focus on the O'Neil family. It was about two young servants employed by them.

Amelia Champlain was a pretty kitchen maid who fell in love with a dashing young man who worked in the stables. His name was Richard Bittle. Amelia had a secret dream to become a famous mystery writer. She shared this dream with no one but Richard.

During one of Richard's late-night visits, Amelia showed him the several unpublished, handwritten novels she kept hidden in her room. She loved telling Richard about her stories, and he was always a captive audience. He believed in her talent and encouraged her to write in all her spare time.

"Someday, my dear Amelia, you will be the most beloved writer in the land," Richard said to her with glowing, admiring eyes.

"With your love and encouragement, I believe I can make anything come true," Amelia answered.

"You must never tell any of the other servants about your writing, Amelia," he warned her. "At the very least

they will tease you, a kitchen maid, for aspiring to such great heights. At the very worst, they will see your talent and try to sabotage your success."

"You are so full of love and advice, Richard," Amelia said as they embraced. *"How would I ever do it without you?"*

"Just promise me you will keep your work a secret until you have completed a manuscript you think will dazzle the publishers. We will announce your triumph to the entire O'Neil family and someday own a manor twice as marvelous as this," Richard said with pride.

Elizabeth's heart began to thump. Where had she come up with such a tale? Then she shook her head—there had to be a reasonable explanation. *Amelia is kind of like me—she dreams of being a writer. And Richard is the necessary love interest to make the story more romantic.* But her explanations ended there. *Where are the details coming from? What do I know about manors, or servants, or the O'Neil family?* It was almost as if something foreign were controlling her mind, or at least her hand.

Elizabeth shivered as she realized that the cabin was pitch-dark. All the lights were out in the cabin, and the sun had set. The glow of the pen had given her all the illumination she had needed to read and write.

Suddenly, she heard a faint pitter-patter on the roof. *It's just a squirrel,* she thought, to console herself, but it was useless. The creaking of the bunk, the rustling of the leaves outside, and the drip of the bathroom faucet were giving her the creeps.

I have to get out of here, she thought. *Maybe I should go meet the gang in the main lodge. I've had more than enough writing for the night*. She was about to push herself off the bunk and turn on the lights when something yanked her hand back to the paper.

As the story continued, it was late one night, and Amelia was in the kitchen with a sheaf of paper. It was a draft of her latest mystery novel. Amelia was filled with excitement as she told Richard that she finally had written a manuscript she was proud enough of to submit to a publishing company in New York.

Amelia placed butter cookies on a china tray and offered them to Richard with a steaming cup of tea.

"It sounds brilliant," Richard told her, nibbling on a cookie. "I imagine that this is just the type of material the publishers are looking for."

"Do you really think so?" Amelia asked modestly. "Oh, Richard, maybe my dream can come true."

"Our dreams, my darling." He kissed her softly on the hand.

"Maybe someday this book will be translated into different languages. That way people all over the would can enjoy it," she said.

"You are radiant with passion," Richard told her admiringly. "I adore the way your cheeks are flushed with excitement."

Richard bade her a loving farewell at the back entrance, and they embraced before he left. Filled with excitement, Amelia funneled her energy into cleaning up the room. She brushed her finger over the spot where his lips had touched the cup before immersing it in the soapy water. She hummed a tune as she swept the floor, nibbling on left-over butter cookies along the way.

Then Amelia turned to get her manuscript—but it was missing. She looked under the table, on the counter, and even in the most unlikely places, like the icebox and cabinets. She ran to the parlor where a housekeeper was dusting, and enlisted her help in the search. But it was all to no avail. Finally, she glanced into the roaring kitchen fire. The title page was at the edge, just starting to char around its corners.

Amelia dropped to the floor and began to weep. Somehow, when she opened the door to let Richard out, the wind must have blown the pages into the fire. Devastated by the loss of her literary masterpiece, Amelia cried herself to sleep. She was grief-stricken that she knew she would never be able to retell the story. It was a total loss. Richard, too, would be shattered.

A tear came to Elizabeth's eye as she completed the passage. Poor Amelia! It was such a tragic story, unlike anything she had ever read before.

Elizabeth examined the pen in the palm of her hand. She had hoped it would help cure her writer's block, but she certainly hadn't imagined *this*. It was almost as though the pen were possessed by some strange power.

Eight

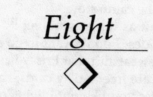

"Bingo! Bingo!" Priscilla yelled in her Southern accent.

It was the tenth and final game of bingo and the second time that Priscilla Westover had managed to win a game in the evening's contest. Her blond curls bounced as she jumped up and down in ecstasy. "I won, I won again! Mommy and Daddy will be so proud."

"She's acting like she just won a vacation to Hawaii," Jessica muttered to Miranda.

Gunnie presented Priscilla with the prize, a green Camp Faraway sweatshirt.

"Oh, thank you, Gunnie. It's absolutely gorgeous," Priscilla said politely. "Mother always says I look good in green." She winked at Gunnie before running back to her seat.

"That's the color *I* wanted," Jessica grunted. "It would look great with my yellow shorts."

"Personally, I like the royal blue. But you can still buy one," Miranda said. "There's probably tons more at the camp store."

"It's just not as fun as winning it," Jessica complained. "Besides, I don't want to go around wearing the same sweatshirt that Prissy has."

"You guys are free to play cards, hang out, read, or do whatever you like until lights out," Lisa, the writing teacher, announced.

But Jessica knew that the fun was over for the night. There was an audition tomorrow, and she had a lot of work to do. She'd brought her script to the lodge so that she could begin rehearsing.

"I'm going back to Windelwisp with Mandy," Miranda said. "You and I won't get any work done if we're rehearsing the play together."

"Good point," Jessica said. *As if she has much rehearsing to do,* she added to herself.

Miranda and Mandy left, as Jessica settled into a comfortable spot close to the blazing fire. She flipped over the cover and stared down at the title page of *The Royal Switch*.

As she read, Jessica was vaguely aware of the chatter going on around her, but the story was so engrossing that she wasn't tempted to look up. The play told of a young peasant named Penelope who was born a princess but raised a pauper—she had been accidentally switched at birth. When the mishap was discovered, Penelope was notified, quickly whisked away from her home, and groomed to be next in line for the throne of England. But the royal life was very different from the farm where she had grown up, and Penelope had a hard time adjusting. She missed her old family so much that she ended up talking the mistaken princess into switching back with her.

Jessica finished the play and sighed contentedly. It was the most wonderful play she had ever read. It was funny and heartwarming and unpredictable all at the same time. *And I'd be absolutely perfect for Penelope.*

Jessica put down the script and got up to get a glass of fruit juice. She had a long night ahead of her. She was determined to get her audition scene down pat, and she'd need every ounce of energy she had.

Well, here goes, Jessica thought, returning to her spot by the fire. *That's weird.* She checked her seat. *I thought I left the script right here.* She looked around on the floor and a table that was close by, but the script was nowhere in sight.

"'Which one is the salad fork?'"

Jessica looked across the room, where Priscilla was reciting Penelope's lines. Priscilla caught Jessica's eye and tossed her head triumphantly.

Hmm, Jessica thought. *Somehow, I don't think that snooty look is in the script—looks like Prissy's got something up her sleeve. I'll bet she's stolen my script so that she has an advantage in tomorrow's tryout!*

Jessica inhaled and strode across the room.

"What's wrong, Jessica?" Priscilla asked in a sugary-sweet tone. "I see you're no longer studying your lines. Are you bored with the play already?"

That was all Jessica needed. "Give it back, Priscilla."

"Give what back?" Priscilla replied innocently.

"You know very well what I'm talking about," Jessica said firmly. "My script!"

Priscilla waved her own script at Jessica. "Why would I bother taking your script when I already have one of my own?"

A few campers crowded around.

"You took it so I wouldn't be able to prepare for the play, Priscilla. It's pretty obvious," Jessica snapped.

"Oh, honestly, Jessica," Priscilla said. "Why should I be threatened by *you*? I'm the spitting image of her, according to the description of her on page one."

Jessica glared at Priscilla. "I wouldn't put anything past you after what you did to Elizabeth in Hangman's Cave."

"I've been sitting here the whole time," Priscilla said, defending herself. "Didn't you see me?" she asked, turning to Nicole, who sat on a nearby couch.

Nicole bit her lip. "She's been sitting there ever since we finished with the songs," she confirmed.

"Maybe you just didn't notice," Jessica said.

"Actually, Jessica," Starr added. "I've been sitting here, too, and Priscilla hasn't gotten up the whole time."

Holly finally approached the group. "What's going on here?" she asked.

Priscilla shook her head with contempt. "Jessica is falsely accusing me of having stolen her script, Holly. It's the rudest thing that anyone has ever done to me. And, of course, everyone here can back up the fact that I haven't even left my seat."

Jessica turned to Holly. "I just got up for a drink, and when I came back it was gone," she explained. "I just thought—" Jessica broke off and glanced at Starr. Maybe it really wasn't fair to have pointed the finger at Priscilla without looking a little harder.

"You're just trying to make me look bad in front of everyone," Priscilla said.

"Why don't we hold a trial," Nicole said.

"Holly could be the judge," Danielle suggested.

"Everyone settle down. We don't need to go to court to settle this." Holly looked at Jessica. "Jessica, come on, let's retrace your steps and see if it doesn't turn up."

Jessica nodded and followed Holly across the lodge, back to the spot where she had been reading.

"It was right here," Jessica said, pointing to the chair. "Whoever heard of a disappearing script?"

Jessica plopped back into the chair, as Holly looked in all the obvious places she had already searched.

"Look at this," Holly said suddenly, pointing at the fireplace.

Jessica peeked into the roaring fireplace. The title page of her script was at the edge of the brick corner. The rest of the script had already gone up in flames.

Jessica shook her head in disbelief. "I don't get it. Who would have . . . ? How . . . ?"

"I don't know. It's pretty weird," Holly said, still staring at the flames.

Jessica sighed in frustration. "Well, whatever. All I know is that auditions are tomorrow, and I don't have a script."

"Maybe one of the others will let you share her script," Holly suggested. "I thought Miranda and Mandy had a copy of their own."

"But they need them to prepare for the audition, too," Jessica said. "And besides, I've lost all my concentration, Holly. I'll never be able to memorize my lines tonight."

"Tell you what," Holly said. "Tomorrow morning after breakfast, I'll get you excused from swimming and horseback riding. Maybe Miranda will let you borrow her script, and you can use the time to prepare yourself."

Jessica bit her lip. "That's not a bad idea."

"I'm sure you'll be ready for the audition by the afternoon," Holly assured her.

Jessica smiled. "Thanks a lot, Holly." Suddenly, a loud crackle from the fireplace caught her attention. Jessica turned to see the title page of *The Royal Switch* igniting, along with the rest of the script.

Nine

"Lizzie? Lizzie, wake up," Jessica said softly.

Elizabeth turned over and slowly opened her eyes. The cabin was dark, and no one was around except for Jessica. It took Elizabeth a moment to figure out where she was. *Oh, yeah,* she remembered. *I came back after dinner by myself, and I must have fallen asleep.* "I had the weirdest dream, Jess," she told her sister as she sat up in bed.

"Oh, yeah? Were you and Johnny Buck skiing together in the Alps?" Jessica asked.

Elizabeth frowned. "*What?*"

"Oh, nothing," Jessica said dismissively. "That was just my dream last night. Or maybe that was the night before . . ."

Elizabeth tucked her tangled hair behind her ears. "Well, my dream took place at Camp Faraway long, long ago. There was this beautiful young housemaid named Amelia Champlain who wanted to be an author. She was in love with Richard Bittle, a stable hand."

Jessica rolled her eyes. "That sounds more like a book than a dream."

Suddenly, Elizabeth felt her chest tighten as it all came back to her. She hadn't dreamed about Amelia and Richard, she had written about them! She put her face in her hands at the sheer horror of the recollection.

"What's your problem?" Jessica asked.

"You're right, Jess—it *is* a book. A story, anyway. I wrote it." Elizabeth dug under the mattress and pulled out the pad of paper.

"You wrote down your dream?" Jessica asked hesitantly.

"No. It was never a dream." Elizabeth clutched the pad to her chest. "I wrote it with the pen."

"So Emerald Lake and your weird glowing pen have finally inspired you, huh?" Jessica grabbed the pad from her and flipped through the pages. "Cool color." Jessica pointed out the bluish lavender of the ink. "But this doesn't even look like your writing," she went on.

"I know. Creepy, isn't it?"

"Yeah, I guess." Jessica shrugged and went over to her trunk.

"Jessica! Don't you think this is freaky? I didn't

write this story," Elizabeth cried, holding up the pad.

Jessica slipped her flannel nightgown over her head. "What do you mean, you didn't write it? Then who did?"

"You just admitted to me that it didn't look like my handwriting," Elizabeth reminded her.

"But it's an old-fashioned pen. Maybe the tip made your writing come out differently," Jessica said, taking a guess. "You've obviously got a terrible headache, and it's causing you to overreact or something."

Elizabeth exhaled loudly. "I don't have a headache, Jessica!"

"Sheesh, so don't bite my head off about it, OK? I mean, you *did* kind of give everyone the idea that you had this horrible headache."

Elizabeth shook her head. "Actually, I wasn't really sick. I just wanted to get some work done on my article about Roland Barge and try out the pen. I faked it so I could do it in privacy."

Jessica cocked an eyebrow. "You? Elizabeth Wakefield, my honest twin sister, pulled a fast one on Holly?"

Elizabeth nodded guiltily. "But now I'm starting to wish I'd never found that pen."

Jessica furrowed her brow. "Let's get this straight. You were doing back flips about that pen the other night, and now you wish you'd never found it?"

Elizabeth groaned. "Will you listen to me, Jess? This isn't just a normal pen. When I sat down to write my article, the pen took me over and just spat out the story about Amelia and Richard. It's like the pen wrote the story for me."

"Oh, come on, Lizzie," Jessica protested. "A pen that writes by itself? Does it talk, too?"

Elizabeth couldn't help smiling. She had to admit, she was starting to sound crazy. "OK, so maybe there *is* some logical explanation," she admitted.

"Of course there is," Jessica agreed. She climbed up and sat beside her sister on the top bunk. "Anyway, you're lucky you got some work done, no matter how it happened." Jessica sighed. "I, on the other hand, had the worst night in the history of the world."

"What happened?" Elizabeth asked sympathetically, anxious to get her mind off the pen.

"I was rehearsing my script by the fireplace, and I got up for some juice," Jessica told her.

"Hmm," Elizabeth murmured, glancing down at her pad of paper. *But I didn't write it, the pen did*, she concluded again. *I was here, I saw it happen*. Then she shook her head and glanced back at her sister.

"When I came back," Jessica continued, "my script was gone." She went on to explain how she had made a fuss and accused Prissy of stealing it. "Finally, Holly helped me try to find it. And here's the clincher, Lizzie: it was burned up in the fireplace."

Elizabeth felt her throat tighten. "The *fireplace*?"

"Yup," Jessica continued. "Holly happened to notice it just before the title page caught on fire. I have no idea how it ended up in there, but everyone swore that Priscilla didn't do it, and I know for a fact that I didn't go near that fire."

Elizabeth felt the blood rush from her face.

"Hey, what's going on? You look kind of ghostly." Jessica studied Elizabeth's face. "Are you sure you aren't really sick?"

Elizabeth opened her mouth, but nothing came out.

"You're really acting weird tonight, Elizabeth. What's going on?" Jessica demanded.

"There's more to the story about Amelia and Richard than I told you," Elizabeth finally said.

"Oh, yeah? Do they have a great wedding or trip to Paris or something?" Jessica asked.

Elizabeth shook her head grimly. "When I left off, Amelia had just completed a mystery novel that she thought she would be able to get published."

Jessica rolled her eyes. "Bor-ing."

"Just listen, Jess. Amelia got up to let Richard out, and when she came back, her book had mysteriously ended up in the fireplace. It was in flames. The only remaining piece was the title page."

"So?" Jessica said.

"Don't you get it, Jessica?" Elizabeth continued.

"That's exactly what happened to you."

"Oh, wow," Jessica said nonchalantly. "What a weird coincidence."

"What if it's not just a coincidence?" Elizabeth asked, raising her eyebrows. "What if the pen was speaking to me, trying to warn me about you?"

"Oh, please, Elizabeth," Jessica said. "You really have been reading too many mysteries. There's no way a pen could have supernatural powers. I bet it had to do with our psychic ability to communicate to each other."

"Give me a break, Jessica," Elizabeth protested. "We don't communicate with each other psychically."

"Well, what about all the times when we unknowingly ordered the exact same ice cream combination at Casey's? How do you explain that?" Jessica asked.

Elizabeth looked at her sister skeptically. "I don't know, Jess—"

"It's like you picked up on my distress and somehow transformed it into a story," Jessica went on.

Elizabeth gave a small smile. "OK, OK. Maybe you're right," she agreed. "That's still kind of spooky, but it probably makes more sense than a pen with a mind of its own."

"How are you feeling, Elizabeth?" Mandy asked, as she and Miranda came into the cabin together.

Elizabeth and Jessica were still sitting next to

each other on Elizabeth's bunk. To Jessica's relief, Elizabeth was no longer going on about her supernatural pen.

"You were out cold when we came in earlier," Miranda told her. "Mandy collided with her trunk, knocked over the lamp, and fell flat on her face, and you didn't even squirm."

Elizabeth nodded. "Well, I'm much, much better," she said, throwing Jessica a glance. "Thanks."

"She slept it off," Jessica said quickly, trying not to smile.

"Good." Miranda turned to Jessica. "I don't know what you did to old Prissy, but she's more determined than ever to get the part of Penelope. Just knowing her, I wouldn't say you had much competition, but you never know."

Jessica frowned in confusion. "You wouldn't say that *I* had much competition? From Priscilla? What about you? Aren't you trying out for Penelope, too?"

"Me?" Miranda asked. "Nah. I mean, I was already Penelope once, so where's the challenge? I'm trying out for Eleanor, the one who ends up with the crown. A very pivotal role. Not as much stage time, but a chance to do an English accent. That's an important tool for any aspiring actress. I've already got the new lines memorized. Hey, what's with you, Jessica? You look like you just swallowed a fish whole or something."

Jessica burst out laughing. "I guess I was just thinking of a friend of mine back home—Lila. She'd want the lead no matter what, even if she'd played it a million times. Just for the sake of playing the lead."

"Jess and Lila have kind of a competition thing going," Mandy confided.

"Well, you won't have to compete with me," Miranda assured her. "Or with Mandy."

"I'm trying out for Prince Joseph," Mandy said in a deep, manly voice.

Jessica giggled. "I think you'll both be awesome."

Miranda reached into her backpack and pulled out her script. "We heard about what happened. Since I already know my lines, I figured you might get some good use out of this."

"Thanks, Miranda," Jessica said, taking the copy. "I'll keep a close eye on it this time."

"Now there's something I'd like to borrow from *you*," Miranda said.

"What?" Jessica asked.

"Your purple walking shorts," Miranda replied. "I think they're just the right look for an audition—dramatic yet sporty."

Jessica smiled as she climbed down from her bunk. "They'd be perfect for you, Madame Eleanor."

Ten

"Everybody will have a chance to try out for the part of her choice," Gunnie said from a director's chair in the back of the theater.

Jessica squirmed in her seat. As Holly had suggested, she had used the morning to prepare. She had learned the scene and could hardly wait to audition.

"There are enough roles for everyone to be cast, and I'll make my decisions immediately afterward. Unfortunately, you may not get the part you wanted, but that's what happens in the real theater world. My choices will be posted on the bulletin board in the hallway."

Each girl had to stand up and say what part she was trying out for. Jessica counted eleven other girls who were vying for the role of Penelope.

"Let's start with Priscilla reading Penelope and Mandy reading Joseph," Gunnie said.

"Break a leg, Mandy," Miranda said with a wink.

Mandy and Priscilla took their places up on the stage, and Jessica braced herself for Penelope's opening line, which she knew so well.

Suddenly, a strange, stunned look came over Priscilla's face. She bit her fingernails and looked out at the crowd.

Mandy glanced nervously at the audience, too, then gave Priscilla a little nudge. Priscilla was still silent.

Looks like Prissy's got a serious case of stage fright, Jessica thought.

Finally, Miranda got up and handed a copy of the script to Priscilla.

Priscilla looked down at the script and began to read from it. "'Exterior, lake, day. Penelope uses a washboard by the lake. She rubs a shirt . . .'"

"That's the stage direction, Priscilla," Mandy chided.

Jessica put her hand over her mouth to cover her tiny grin.

"Your lines start right there." Mandy pointed to the place on the script.

"Oh, of course." Priscilla cleared her throat. "'Young man! You've startled me,'" she read stiffly from the page.

"'Actually, I'm a prince,'" Mandy said in a masculine voice.

"'But I—I didn't kiss a frog,'" Priscilla sputtered.

"'Sorry to disappoint you, but I'm not that kind of prince. The truth is, I'm your brother,'" Mandy continued.

"'Take me away to your *castle*? But this is my *home*. The *farm* is my castle,'" Priscilla said overdramatically.

"Priscilla. You skipped a page," Mandy said with frustration.

As the girls auditioned, Gunnie took a few notes on her clipboard. "Thank you very much, girls. Mandy, why don't you stay up there and continue reading Joseph. Jessica, why don't you take your turn as Penelope."

Priscilla tossed her blond curls. "But I'd like to do it again."

Gunnie shook her head. "Everybody gets one turn, Priscilla. You did a fine job. Jessica's up now."

Priscilla stormed off, her chin raised high in the air.

Jessica squeezed Miranda's hand before going up to the stage. She adjusted her top and looked out at Gunnie for her cue.

"Begin when you're ready," Gunnie told them.

You can do it, Jessica, she said to herself as she took her place and imagined she was sweet Penelope, being informed of her royal status.

Jessica put her hand to her chest and looked at Mandy beseechingly. She began to protest Prince Joseph's declaration of her royal stature.

"'But I'm at home on the farm. I milk the cows and make fresh pie every day. I don't belong at a castle,'" Jessica said with passion.

"'At this point you probably don't,'" Mandy responded. "But according to your birthright, you do.'"

"'But you can't force me to leave. My life is here. My family. My friends.'" A tear came to Jessica's eye.

"'A princess doesn't cry in public. That's rule number one.'"

Jessica started to bawl.

"'Boy, do I have my work cut out for me,'" Mandy replied, giving her a handkerchief.

Jessica took the hanky and blew her nose loudly.

"'Rule number two. A princess does not blow her nose in public,'" Mandy went on.

"'Is there anything I *can* do in public?'" Jessica wept again.

Mandy paused and scratched her head. "'You may breathe.'"

Jessica let out an enormous breath, broken by sniffles and sobs.

"Thank you, Jessica," said Gunnie with no discernible inflection. "Nicole, you're up."

Elizabeth sat at her desk in journalism class and stared at a blank piece of notebook paper. She could hear the sound of pencils scribbling against the nearby desk surfaces. It seemed as though everyone but she was focused on her article.

As hard as she tried to concentrate on Roland Barge, Elizabeth could think of nothing but the red pen and the strange story about Richard and Amelia.

She looked up in frustration. On the chalkboard Lisa had written the word RESEARCH in block letters. *Maybe that's it,* Elizabeth thought suddenly. *Maybe if I got more into the article, I could forget about the pen for a while. I don't know enough about Roland Barge. How can I write an accurate article if I don't have enough details about my subject?*

Lisa was wandering through the aisles, looking over the shoulders of her students. A pencil was tucked behind her ear.

"Lisa?" Elizabeth asked when she came by her desk, "would it be all right if I went over to the library? I'd like to find out a bit more about Roland Barge before I begin. The biography I checked out yesterday doesn't seem to be enough for me."

Lisa smiled. "As I said earlier, research is one of the best ways to get you over a hump in your writing. There's still plenty of time left this period. Why don't you check out some materials and bring them back?"

"Good idea," Elizabeth said eagerly, standing up. "I'll be back in a flash."

*   *   *

The whole class gathered in the hallway around the bulletin board where Gunnie had posted her selections.

Miranda and Mandy had somehow ended up at the very front of the cluster, while Jessica was stuck in the back. They high-fived and ran over to Jessica.

"Well?" Jessica eagerly asked.

"I got Eleanor," Miranda proudly announced.

"And I got Joseph," Mandy added. "I was a total shoo-in, seeing as I was the only one to try out."

"Congrats, you guys," Jessica said, her heart beating wildly. "Did you see if—"

"Well, catch you later, Jess," Miranda interrupted.

"We want to see if we can get a look at the costumes," Mandy added as they ran back toward the auditorium.

Jessica suddenly felt her stomach knot. Were they hiding something from her? Did she get cast as one of the evil sisters or the matronly queen? Jessica anxiously tried to push her way up.

"The maid!" Priscilla hollered just as Jessica reached the front. "I refuse to play the maid! This is unjust!" she cried, running back into the theater.

Jessica leaned toward the list and squinted to make out the tiny writing. Bold letters at the top of the sheet read: PENELOPE—JESSICA WAKEFIELD.

Jessica stared at the list for a moment in shock. It was too good to be true.

"Way to go, Jessica," Tracy told her, patting her on the back.

"I knew you'd get Penelope," Nicole added. "Your audition was totally amazing. How do you manage to be so funny and emotional at the same time?"

Jessica smiled graciously. "It's all a matter of being true to yourself," she replied, quoting from something she'd read about acting somewhere.

She turned around and calmly walked back to the theater. After all, she was the star—she had to show poise and charm.

Miranda and Mandy were waiting in the entryway when she came back inside the auditorium.

"All right, Jess!" Miranda exclaimed.

"You could have told me, you know," Jessica complained.

"We just wanted to see you sweat it out," Mandy admitted.

"You shouldn't be too spoiled so early in your career," Miranda added.

Elizabeth placed the stack of articles about Roland Barge on her desk. She'd found and photocopied a dozen old newspaper articles about the famous author and couldn't wait to read every word of them. *I'm sure there's some really interesting material here,* she thought.

Trying to decide where to begin, Elizabeth

flipped through the copies and admired a small photograph of Roland at age twenty-five. His chiseled chin and cropped dark hair were striking. Eagerly, she began to read the accompanying interview.

After just a few paragraphs, Elizabeth was disappointed. Roland Barge came off as a conceited dilettante. He refused to talk about his past. He would only gush over his novels, without giving a clue about his personal life.

Elizabeth moved on to the next article. It portrayed Roland Barge as an angry man with a violent temper. Another mentioned that he was missing an eye but didn't say why. *But his written words are really what's important*, Elizabeth reasoned. *Whoever said that a famous writer has to be a good guy, too?* She decided to focus on some old literary reviews she had dug up.

Roland Barge's early books, such as *Death of a Hangman*, had received raves. "Gripping, textured, unpredictable," one review read. "Roland Barge has done it again," said a review of *Skeleton Island*. "The only predictability in a Barge novel," it went on, "is that every page will reveal new wonders and excitement." Only his final novel, *Death on a Mountain Top*, was negatively received. One journalist wrote, "It is as though he lost his talent overnight. The story is grossly incompetent, with an implausible ending and an uncompelling hero."

Starr tapped Elizabeth's shoulder. "Elizabeth?" she said. "Are you OK?"

Elizabeth looked up. "Sure—why?"

"You have an awful scowl on your face," Starr remarked.

"I do?" Elizabeth patted her cheeks. "I guess I'm just shocked, Starr. I thought I admired Roland Barge, but these articles make him sound like an awful person."

"What do you mean?" Starr asked.

"Well, he seems like a total grouchy recluse," Elizabeth began. "He never admitted what influenced him to become a writer. He never hung out in any literary circles like the other big writers of his time. He was a total hermit. But he was a millionaire. This article says that his early books were translated into almost every language. He made a fortune from the publishers. But he hardly spent a dime of the money."

"Retirement savings or something?" Starr joked.

Elizabeth shrugged. "No one really knows a thing about his retirement. At the end of his career, when he had lost all respect as an author, people really started hating him. One night he just disappeared. No one ever found out what happened to him."

"'Something is rotten in the state of Denmark,'" Starr quoted. "That's from *Hamlet*."

Elizabeth put a finger over her lips. "You know, I wonder . . ."

"You wonder what?" Starr asked.

Elizabeth shook her head. "Maybe I'm getting carried away, but I just had this thought. What if he was murdered?"

"Murdered?" Starr said grimly.

"He had a lot of enemies," Elizabeth explained with uneasiness.

Lisa stood before the class. "OK, everybody, class is dismissed. Rough drafts are due tomorrow."

"I think I'll stick around," Elizabeth said to Starr. "I still have a lot of reading to do. Want to stay, too?"

"Can't. I've just compiled all the questions I'm going to ask Holly. She's agreed to meet me at Windelwisp before dinner for the interview," Starr said. Then her voice dropped. "Besides, to tell you the truth, all this murder talk is kind of giving me the creeps."

Elizabeth smiled wryly. "Yeah, I know what you mean. Oh, well, I'll see you later."

As Starr and the rest of the students gradually cleared out, Elizabeth glanced at Lisa, who was gathering her things in the back of the classroom. "Do you mind if I stay for a while, Lisa? I'd like to keep working."

"I'm always happy to see a dedicated student. Just be sure you turn out the lights when you leave," Lisa replied.

Once Lisa was gone, Elizabeth let out a satisfied sigh. She could definitely bang out a rough draft in the quiet classroom.

Elizabeth read the last of the interviews and decided she would jot down a brief outline for her story. *I guess I could start by discussing his early works*, she thought. But after she wrote down a few words, she started to tune out. Her mind drifted to the strange tale of Amelia and Richard. There was so much more to know about them. The life of Roland Barge seemed dull and trivial in comparison.

The article can wait, Elizabeth decided. She pushed the copies aside so that she could take a stab at continuing with the love story. She flipped to a clean sheet of paper and tapped her pencil on the desk. When she had left off, Amelia was in tears over the loss of her prized manuscript. But what should happen next? How could Amelia deal with the tragedy? Would Richard come to console her with flowers? Somehow, Elizabeth couldn't think of a thing to write.

Elizabeth got up and paced through the room the way she heard great writers did when they were at a loss for words. But *nothing* came to her. She sat back down and doodled Amelia's and Richard's names on the pad, but then she stopped—she had nothing more to say.

Elizabeth stared at the pencil in her hands, and

suddenly she knew what the problem was. As interested as she was in the story of Richard and Amelia, she wasn't the one who composed it. Now she was more certain than ever—the power was all in the pen.

Eleven

◇

Elizabeth squirmed in her bed all night long as thoughts of Amelia and Richard filtered through her mind. Finally, she felt an electric force dragging her hand toward the edge of her bed. *The pen,* she thought. *It's calling me again.* She dug underneath the mattress, where she had stashed her things.

Elizabeth marveled at the pen's fluorescent glow and hid under the covers to make sure it didn't wake anyone. The moment it touched the pad, the story resumed. The words flowed out more quickly than ever, despite Elizabeth's fatigue.

When Amelia arrived home from an afternoon of strawberry picking with her kitchen friends, Franny and Gretchen, she found a note by the pots and pans.

Richard's messy writing was easily identifiable, and she opened it with eager anticipation.

> My darling Amelia,
>   Every moment I am without you I am un-
> happy and lonely. Please meet me on the lake
> this evening at half past eight.
>   With love and affection,
>   Richard

Amelia clutched the letter to her chest. She had been in a sour mood ever since the incident with the fireplace. A year of hard work had been taken from her within seconds. But the note brought a smile to her face. Richard's love would save her from the anguish. She could hardly wait for their meeting and counted the hours until she would be in his arms.

Before setting out toward Emerald Lake, Amelia primped her hair, put on her Sunday best, and gathered a small basket of strawberries to give Richard.

She left through the back entrance of the manor. Amelia felt a drizzle in the air. The sky above was filled with clouds, and a storm seemed to be coming. Would it be wise to depart under such conditions? Amelia was wary, but her overwhelming desire to be by Richard's side won out over logic, and she scurried on her way.

At the lake, Amelia untied her rowboat from the dock and got in. Adjusting the oars, she set out for their meeting spot. She was just minutes away from being with

Richard—her heart pounded in anticipation. Perhaps this was the night he would profess his deep affection for her and propose marriage. Amelia dreamed about the wonderful life they would have together. They would travel the world and raise a small family. His love would inspire her to move on from her tragic loss and to write more books. There were many other mystery stories she could tell. With Richard's encouragement and admiration, the possibilities seemed endless.

Amelia rowed out toward the middle of the lake, where they would reunite. She looked up at the storm clouds and felt at ease. If anything were to happen, Richard would surely be there to save her.

Amelia looked around, wondering what was keeping him. Perhaps he thought the clouds looked too dense and had used his better judgment to stay away. He must have thought Amelia too sensible to risk herself to such conditions. As Amelia pondered going back to shore, her boat suddenly started filling with water. Somewhere in the wooden siding there was a leak. Scrambling to bail out the boat with her hands, she heard the sound of thunder in the distance. Suddenly, the torrential storm hit, and Amelia was washed overboard. She clambered for the boat, but it was hopeless. It had already begun to sink below the surface.

Elizabeth jerked her hand from the page. The hairs on the back of her neck stood on end. *Where is this stuff coming from?* she wondered. *It's as if the pen has a soul of its own.* Though she had stopped writing, the pen seemed to be pulsating in her hand. *It can't be—it's impossible. Everyone knows pens aren't alive.* She put the pen down, and the glow slowly faded. It sat there like an ordinary pen.

Elizabeth huddled under the covers, thinking of Amelia and Richard. What was going on? Somehow her love story had turned into a gruesome thriller. She looked over at Jessica, who was sleeping soundly. *Should I wake her?* She quickly brushed the thought aside. *I can't wake Jessica just because of a story.* After all, Amanda Howard's stories had often frightened her, too, and she'd always toughed it out.

Elizabeth pulled the covers tight around her and closed her eyes. But she couldn't get the thought of Amelia out of her mind. Had she survived the storm? Automatically, Elizabeth picked up the pen and touched the pad of paper.

Amelia thrashed around in the stormy lake. The choppy water kept sending waves over her head, and she choked on a mouthful of water. It seemed there was no hope, that she would never make it back to shore alive.

Suddenly, out of nowhere, Amelia noticed a search-light nearby.

My Richard has come to rescue me, *she thought as she struggled to tread water.*

She used all her strength to wave her hands over her

head. "Richard," she yelled. "Richard, save me!"

The boat was on its way to her rescue in the middle of the lake. But the turbulence of the water made it a rocky journey, and it seemed forever until the boat was by her side.

"Help me!" she yelled. "Please, Richard. I'm right here." She bobbed up and down in the water.

As the boat reached her, Amelia was too weak and worn out to look at her rescuer's face—to discover that he wasn't Richard at all but a young fisherman with a scruffy beard and strong hands.

Though his boat was large and sturdy, saving Amelia was dangerous under the rough conditions. He tossed her a life preserver attached to a rope and pulled her as close to the boat as he could. He went to the edge of the rail and nearly lost his balance as a soaring current of water passed beneath them. Finally, using all his strength, he was able to drag Amelia from the lake.

When the fisherman pulled Amelia into his boat, she was almost lifeless.

"Richard," Amelia cried. "Oh, Richard, darling, you're my savior," she exclaimed as she collapsed into the fisherman's arms.

The fisherman put Amelia in the cabin down below and covered her with woolen blankets. He let her sleep while he went to investigate her boat and find out what had happened. By this time, the storm was tapering off, and they were no longer in danger.

Amelia was startled to awaken to the face of a

stranger. "Where is Richard?" she gasped.

"You must not remember— No, of course you don't." The fisherman broke off and introduced himself, then told her the story of her rescue. He sailed them back to land and escorted Amelia to the manor. The storm was long gone, but the roads were treacherous and muddy, and the trip was exhausting.

"You saved my life. Had you not come along, I can only imagine what my fate might have been. How ever can I thank you?" Amelia asked.

The fisherman smiled at her kindly. "You can thank me by being more careful in the future," he replied.

Amelia looked ashamed. "Perhaps in the future I will use better judgment when I go for an evening cruise. And I suppose my old boat was long overdue to be repaired. It was careless of me."

The fisherman put his hand on her shoulder. "Madam, it wasn't the storm that threw you over. Your boat was sabotaged," he explained.

"Sabotaged!" Amelia exclaimed with alarm.

The fisherman spoke calmly. "There were punctures from a knife along the side of the boat. Someone wanted to see you dead."

Amelia turned pale with fear. "But who ever would want to see me dead?"

Elizabeth dropped the pen, and chills ran up and down her spine. Who could have sabotaged Amelia's boat? Who wanted to see her dead? Was it

one of the servants? The O'Neils? The wind whis-
tled through the trees outside the window, and
Elizabeth felt an inexplicable pang of dread.

"Is that my sister?" Jessica asked Miranda the
next morning as the girls got ready for breakfast.
She pointed to the lump under the covers of
Elizabeth's bunk. "This is a first. Elizabeth
Wakefield, Morning Person of America, sleeps
through Gunnie's deafening wake-up call."

"It's a first for *anyone*," Miranda agreed.

Holly went over to Elizabeth's bed. "Let's get a
move on, Elizabeth," she said, as she pulled off the
pillow that was guarding Elizabeth from the daylight.

"Five more minutes," Elizabeth moaned to
Holly, putting the pillow back over her face.

Miranda raised her eyebrows at Jessica. "Have you
two switched identities overnight or something?"

Jessica giggled. "All I know is, *I* can't sleep in
when there's a play to rehearse for. As for my sister—" Jessica dashed over to her sister's side and
hummed Gunnie's wake-up tune into her ear. "'Its
seven o'clock and it's time to get up, up, up and
start the day with a smile. . . .'"

"Stop it, Jessica," Elizabeth said irritably.

"Oooh, moody, are we?" Jessica teased, leaning
up against the bunk. "What happened to you?"

"I didn't sleep well," Elizabeth groaned.

Jessica pulled off the pillow and looked at Elizabeth. "Look at those bags under your eyes. You look like a wreck."

"Thanks, Jess, I feel much better now," Elizabeth replied.

"Did you get another bad headache?" Miranda asked. "Maybe you should go over to the infirmary for some medicine."

"No, I'm not sick," Elizabeth said wearily.

"Roland Barge giving you nightmares?" Starr asked as she peered at Elizabeth.

Elizabeth sighed as she rolled over. "Something like that."

Twelve

"The Lakeside Serenade is my absolute favorite activity in the whole session of camp," Holly told the girls during dinner. "Second only to the tour of Hangman's Cave, of course."

Gunnie's morning speech had included an announcement that the Lakeside Serenade would take place that evening. It had been the topic of conversation at breakfast, lunch, and now dinner.

"Anything would be better than going back to that creepy old cave," Jessica said.

"I'm with you," Starr agreed.

"So what do we have to do?" Elizabeth asked, yawning. She still hadn't recovered from her late-night writing session.

Holly's eyes lit up with excitement. "Everybody gets a candle, and we sing all the camp songs on the docks of Emerald Lake. And we're in luck, weatherwise—the forecast calls for the most beautiful night of the summer, warm and clear, with a gentle breeze."

Miranda smiled dreamily. "It sounds breathtaking. I'm going to bring my camera."

"Good. I've always looked nice by candlelight," Jessica said, striking a pose.

"You've got free time until then," Holly reminded them, "so do your own thing."

Jessica looked at Mandy and Miranda. "We've got play rehearsal until then."

"Did you memorize all your lines, Jess?" Mandy asked.

"Oh, yeah. Piece of cake," Jessica replied confidently.

Elizabeth yawned again. "I think I'll head back for a nap."

"A nap?" Starr raised her eyebrows. "You're no fun. I say we hang out in the lodge. Once and for all, I'm going to teach you the camp songs. Aren't you getting sick of mumbling your way through?"

Jessica giggled. "Thanks, Starr, you'll be doing a favor for us all," she teased.

Elizabeth flushed slightly. All she really wanted to do was sleep, but she didn't want to be known as the biggest party pooper at Camp Faraway. Plus, anything that would keep her mind off the pen was worth trying. "OK," she told Starr. "Let's go."

*   *   *

" 'Princess Penelope, I've also been instructed by the Prince to burn your raggedy old clothing,' " Priscilla said, lunging toward Jessica.

Jessica and Priscilla were center stage. Jessica stepped away in alarm. " 'But this is my favorite frock,' " she cried.

" 'Trust me, it's a fashion no. Burlap has been out for decades.' " Priscilla chased her across the stage.

" 'But this is my favorite frock,' " Jessica screamed.

"Jessica, you already said that line!" Gunnie yelled from the back of the theater.

Jessica reddened. "Oh—right. Sorry, Gunnie."

"And Priscilla, remember, you're the maid, not part of the royal family. Your walk is too refined."

"It's hard to go against my natural posture, Gunnie," Priscilla protested.

"You're an actor, Priscilla. You're supposed to *become* your part," Gunnie told her. "Now, let's take it from the top of the scene."

Priscilla scurried off the stage, and Jessica plopped down on the canopy bed off to the side.

" 'Come in, Priscilla.' I mean, uh, 'Come in, Miss Wellington,' " Jessica said.

Priscilla dramatically pantomimed the opening of a door and waltzed into the imaginary room. She approached Jessica and examined her hair.

" 'My, my, we're going to have to sterilize every part of you,' " Priscilla said with vengeance, looking distastefully at Jessica. "'I've been ordered by Prince Joseph to do the deed.'"

"Cut!" Gunnie yelled. "Priscilla, you're supposed to adore Princess Penelope. She's a breath of fresh air compared with Eleanor. Remember?"

"Oh, right," Priscilla agreed, as though she had just remembered.

"Continue," Gunnie said, sighing.

"'My, my, we're going to have to sterilize every part of you,'" Jessica said.

"That's Priscilla's line, Jessica," Gunnie said impatiently.

Jessica covered her mouth with her hand. *If those are the maid's lines, what are Penelope's?* Suddenly, her mind was a total blank. In a panic she stared out at the audience and caught Miranda's eyes. It looked as though Miranda was mouthing her the lines, but she couldn't make them out.

"What's going on here?" Gunnie demanded.

Jessica shrugged sheepishly. Miranda had warned her that Penelope was a demanding role. And with swim class, horseback riding, and all her other activities, there had been little time to memorize the entire part. "I have the first act down, Gunnie, I'm just having a *little* trouble with this scene."

"I expected you to have the play memorized by tonight," Gunnie said sternly.

"Hmm," Priscilla grunted with satisfaction. Jessica gave her a glare in return.

"I do. I mean, I will . . . I . . ." Jessica stuttered.

"You carry the weight of the production, Jessica. Everybody is depending on you." Gunnie looked around at the rest of her students, waiting in the stalls. "And it's not just Jessica. You all are going to have to do better than this if *The Royal Switch* is going to come off properly. We have a dress rehearsal tomorrow, and by then I expect all the problems to be ironed out."

Elizabeth and Starr settled onto the couch by the fireplace, and Elizabeth tucked her legs beneath her. The heat emanating from the flames was cozy, and the cushioned sofa was soft and plush, but somehow she was unable to relax. She couldn't forget about Richard and Amelia and the magical pen.

"So how's your article going, Elizabeth?" Starr asked, disrupting Elizabeth's thoughts. "You've hardly talked about it."

"I haven't even written the first paragraph," Elizabeth admitted, nestling up against the arm of the couch. She sighed. "My dream was to come to camp and write a whole mystery novel, but I can't even write a three-page article."

Starr tilted her head and turned to Elizabeth. "'Tis not the point of a young girl's life to fill it up with personal strife."

"Let me guess," Elizabeth said. *"Much Ado About Nothing?"*

"Nope. I just made it up." Starr smiled proudly. "You really think it sounds Shakespearean?"

Elizabeth chuckled. "Sure—you're a real poet, that's for sure."

"Oh, thank you, thank you. Anyway, what I mean is that the point of camp is to have fun, not to get caught up with writing an article," Starr explained.

Elizabeth smiled. "I guess you're right." But the article was actually the least of Elizabeth's worries. What was a little writer's block compared with all the mysterious things that had been happening lately because of the pen?

"Of course I'm right," Starr declared, propping her feet up on a footstool.

Elizabeth glanced at her friend and suddenly had an impulse to tell her everything. *Starr's so smart and insightful—maybe she'd have a good explanation for what's happening with the pen. It's worth a shot, anyway—it's better than keeping it to myself.*

Elizabeth took a deep breath. "Starr, there's something I—" Elizabeth's voice caught. Her heart was pounding at just the thought of telling the story of the pen.

"What?" Starr asked, leaning forward. "You're scaring me."

"I, well, I—" Elizabeth began again. "It's just that I—" At that moment, Elizabeth saw the look of terror in Starr's eyes. *Everything scares Starr,*

Elizabeth remembered. *Amanda Howard's novels make her skin crawl, she was petrified in Hangman's Cave, and she could barely sleep after Gunnie mentioned the murders that supposedly took place at the campground. Starr would be terrified if I told her about the pen.*

"What is it, Elizabeth?" Starr pressed, despite her obvious fear.

"I, um, need some punch or something. Yeah, some punch. I'm really thirsty," Elizabeth blurted out. "You want some?"

Starr laughed. "I've never seen anyone so nervous about wanting some punch. I feel bad—I should have let you take a nap. The lack of sleep is obviously getting to you."

"Yeah, I guess," Elizabeth mumbled.

"Listen, you need to chill out. Stay here, and I'll get the punch," Starr offered.

"Thanks, Starr," Elizabeth said softly.

While Starr headed for the counter of refreshments, Elizabeth stared off into the flames. *Forget about the pen*, she urged herself, *push it out of your mind.* Elizabeth listened to the crackling of the logs and watched the little orange sparks evaporate into the air. She remembered the fire in the story—how it had consumed Amelia's novel. *And Jessica's script burned in the fire, too. What did it mean?* Elizabeth wanted badly to believe that what happened to Jessica was just a coincidence, that it had nothing to do with the story she was composing—but what if it did? What if the story about Amelia kept coming true?

"Here you are, Elizabeth." Starr returned with a big glass of punch. "Hey, I thought I told you to chill out," she teased. "You look like you just saw a ghost. What's wrong?"

Elizabeth forced a smile as she took the glass from Starr. "Oh, nothing. I guess I'm still bugged by that article, but I'll be OK. How about if you teach me the camp songs now?"

"Well, OK. The first one . . ." Starr seemed distracted by something through the window.

"Starr?" Elizabeth said. "What's up?"

"Oh, sorry," Starr said, turning back to Elizabeth. "It's just that it looks like it's going to rain. It's weird. Holly said we were supposed to have great weather, remember? Oh, well, I guess those weather people don't know everything, right?"

"Rain?" Elizabeth gasped. Her heart was racing. Amelia almost drowned in an unexpected storm— would the same thing happen in real life? Elizabeth suddenly felt sick as she glanced at the flames leaping in the fireplace. *The fire had consumed Amelia's manuscript—and Jessica's script. Amelia nearly died in a storm—what if Jessica—?*

Elizabeth jumped up from the couch and looked out the window. She could see in the distance that storm clouds were quickly moving in. "You're right," she said, leaning up against the glass.

"Bad news, guys." Holly appeared in the doorway. "There was just a thunderstorm warning on the radio."

Starr let out a frustrated sigh. "Of all nights."

"The serenade has to be postponed until tomorrow. Why don't you stay put in here, and we'll get a game going. I'll round up the rest of the gang."

As Holly rushed on, Elizabeth felt her heart contract in fear. "I've got to get to Emerald Lake," she exclaimed suddenly.

Starr frowned. "But Holly said—"

But Elizabeth was already dashing for the door.

"Elizabeth! What are you thinking?" Starr yelled after her. "You'll get drenched out there."

Without responding, Elizabeth ran from the lodge and sprinted against the wind toward Emerald Lake. She felt a light drizzle in the air, but by the time she made it to the docks, the rain was coming down hard, and she was soaked.

Fog was rolling in, and she looked around for a sign of Jessica. *That's her!* Elizabeth's heart was thundering as she made out the faint figure of her sister far off in the center of the lake. It looked as though she was trying to row back toward the docks.

"Jessica! Jessica!" Elizabeth screamed at the top of her lungs, but the noise of the storm drowned out her cry.

Elizabeth could tell that Jessica was struggling against the current. She watched in horror as one of the oars slipped from her sister's grip. Jessica frantically leaned over to retrieve it, but it floated off in the waves. She tried to move on with the remaining oar, but the fierce wind caused the boat to drift in the opposite direction.

Lightning streaked through the sky.

How could I have been so stupid? Elizabeth asked herself. *How could I have missed the pen's warning?* The story was replaying itself. Like Amelia's, Jessica's boat would begin to sink at any moment. But there was no fisherman on the lake. Elizabeth was the only one who could save her from drowning.

As the cloud cover became denser, Elizabeth lost sight of her sister. "Jessica, where are you?" she yelled.

Elizabeth heard muted shouts coming from behind her, calling her back, but she ignored them. She had to save Jessica.

Elizabeth slipped on the mud and slid all the way to the end of the dock. She frantically pulled off her shoes and dove into the water. She swam furiously toward the center of the lake, but it was a struggle going against the rough current. Losing strength, she choked on water as the waves crashed overhead. As Elizabeth coughed, a strong force sucked her to the depths of the lake. She was pulled all the way to the floor. Her lungs burned. Feeling the bottom with her bare feet, Elizabeth sprang back up with all her might.

Gasping and dizzy once she reached the surface, she barely had the energy to tread water. She looked around desperately for her sister, but the storm obscured her vision. *I won't give up—I have to save her,* she said to herself, trying to muster up every last bit of strength. Finally, she swam on.

Elizabeth suddenly noticed a glare in the distance. It appeared to be a searchlight atop a boat. The boat was headed toward the center of the lake, where she had last sighted Jessica. Though she was still gasping for breath and shivering from the cold water, Elizabeth felt a surge of relief. Jessica would be saved.

The clouds rolled out as quickly as they had rolled in, but the turbulent water made it hard to stay afloat. Elizabeth treaded water as she watched her sister being pulled into the vessel.

But the boat clearly hadn't sighted Elizabeth, and she was far from shore.

Elizabeth shook her hands over her head. "Help! Help me!" she screamed as a force sucked her down again.

Elizabeth bobbed back up to the surface and continued to cry for help. "Over here," she cried, her teeth chattering.

She looked toward the shore and saw Starr,

Miranda, and a group of counselors shouting for her.

"Hang on, Elizabeth!" she thought she heard Starr cry.

"Help is on the way," Holly yelled.

The boat finally made its way toward her.

"Hold on, Elizabeth!" Jessica screamed from the boat.

"Hurry!" Elizabeth exclaimed, struggling to keep her head above the waves.

A life preserver was tossed out to her, and she scrambled toward it. She clutched the preserver with all her might, and she was towed toward the boat.

A strong pair of fisherman's hands pulled her over the side to safety.

"Thank you. You saved me," Elizabeth said to the burly fisherman as she coughed up water. She nearly collapsed from exhaustion. The fisherman helped her regain her balance.

"Lizzie!" Jessica exclaimed, throwing her arms around her sister.

"J-Jess!" Elizabeth stuttered. Her hands and feet were so numb from the cold, she could barely feel them.

As the fisherman returned to the stern, the twins huddled together. Jessica, still drenched, had wrapped herself up in an old woolen blanket. Her lips were purple and her nose was red from the cold. "What happened? How did you end up in the lake?" she asked, spreading part of the blanket over Elizabeth.

"I was about to ask you the same question," Elizabeth replied breathlessly. "Why did you go out on the lake in the first place? You know it's not allowed."

Jessica shrugged. "Well, it was such a beautiful night, and I needed to go over my lines somewhere quiet, so I just thought this once—"

"Oh, Jess!" Elizabeth scolded, shaking her head. "We both could have drowned, you know. Didn't you see the storm clouds?"

"I swear, Elizabeth, there wasn't a cloud in the sky when I started out," Jessica insisted. "All the stars were shining. And what a dramatic setting for rehearsing Penelope, you know? I just couldn't resist."

"That's no excuse." Elizabeth frowned.

"You of all people should be able to understand being overwhelmed by beauty. And, I mean, if I had known there was a storm coming, I never would have done it. When it started to drizzle, I realized I should get back to shore."

"And then you dropped the oar into the water?" Elizabeth asked.

Jessica shuddered. "When I tried to fish it out, I . . . I noticed there was a huge puncture in the boat."

"A puncture?" Elizabeth gasped, recalling the knife gashes in the side of Amelia's boat.

"Water just started spilling in, and the boat started to sink," Jessica explained with a terrified expression. "Just as I fell overboard, the big boat appeared out of nowhere. I don't know what would have happened if he hadn't come along."

"I would have saved you," Elizabeth told her.

Jessica raised her eyebrows. "Is that why you ended up in the lake? You were trying to rescue me?"

Elizabeth nodded. "What did you think I was doing? Taking an evening swim?"

"But how did you know I was in danger?" Jessica asked.

"Well . . . you see . . ." Elizabeth broke off. She was too weak to argue with her sister anymore over the powers of the pen. "It's the twin thing," she finished. "I had a sense of your distress when I was in the lodge with Starr."

"See? I told you we had special powers to communicate with each other." Jessica flashed a satisfied smile. "You know, Lizzie, with you around, I feel like nothing bad could ever happen to me."

Elizabeth smiled weakly as the boat neared the dock. Elizabeth's fingers and toes had regained feeling, but she continued to shiver.

"Here, take the blanket," Jessica offered. "You look like you're freezing." Jessica wrapped it around her sister's shoulders.

But Elizabeth knew that she wasn't shaking from the cold. More than ever, she feared the pen and its mysterious powers. Amelia's and Jessica's lives had now made more than one connection. What would happen next?

Thirteen

"May I take your order, ladies?" Mandy joked, holding an imaginary waiter's pad in the air.

"Our *what*?" Elizabeth asked as she slid into a bench in the cafeteria.

Miranda smiled. "Mandy and I are here to serve you—it's the least we can do to show how glad we are that you guys are all right. We could have lost you last night."

Elizabeth sighed. Ever since the close call on the lake, Elizabeth and Jessica had become celebrities. Everyone wanted to lend them a hand, and numerous girls they had never even met had expressed their relief over their safe return to shore. Holly had reprimanded Jessica severely for breaking one of the camp rules, but after a while even she relented and commended both twins for their bravery and toughness.

"So what'll it be?" Mandy prompted.

"Hmm," Jessica murmured thoughtfully. "How's the French toast?"

"That must have been the most frightening experience of your lifetime," Nicole mused, as she stopped at their table. "You guys are unbelievably brave. I would have run home first thing this morning if I had been you."

"You have no idea how frightening it was," Jessica said, her voice shaking slightly. "The water was close to freezing, and the storm caused these enormous tidal waves. I was moments—moments—away from drowning."

Elizabeth rolled her eyes. *Typical overdramatic Jessica. All this attention probably makes almost drowning worth it.*

Nicole turned toward Elizabeth. "That was so noble of you to risk your life for Jessica," she went on.

Elizabeth stifled another sigh. She wished everyone would stop making such a fuss—she wanted to forget all about that creepy incident on the lake. "Actually, it was no big deal," she mumbled.

"No big deal?" Jessica said. "You nearly froze to death. You didn't even thaw out until this morning."

" 'And thereby hangs a tale,' " Starr said, joining the group of fans.

"Um . . . ?" Jessica said.

"*As You Like It,*" Starr replied. "I think there's a story behind this. I'm going to have to write a piece for the camp paper on you two."

"I'd be happy to do an interview anytime, Starr." Jessica crossed her legs. "Provided you can schedule it between my play rehearsals."

"That'll be great, Jessica. I'm not exactly sure what angle I should take. I mean, should I concentrate on the momentous rescue or the intuition that Elizabeth had of you drowning on the lake?" Starr tapped her fingers.

"It'll be old news by the time the paper comes out, Starr. Let's forget it," Elizabeth pleaded.

"You don't have to be modest, Elizabeth," Mandy told her. "What you did was nothing less than heroic. Anyway, Jessica, anything with the French toast?"

"Just make sure you ask for extra butter and syrup," Jessica instructed.

"So what's it going to be for our hero, the brave Elizabeth?" Miranda asked, smiling. "I bet I can get the cooks to make you a cheese omelet."

Elizabeth reddened. "Listen, you guys, I really don't think—"

"Or do you eat omelets?" Mandy interrupted. "Maybe you'd like pancakes instead?"

"I just don't—"

"I think Elizabeth's in the mood for pancakes," Jessica broke in. "Her forehead always wrinkles like that when she's got a craving for pancakes. Right, Elizabeth?"

Elizabeth shot a look at her sister. "Jessica, I—"

"With a side of fresh fruit," Jessica added. "And a tall glass of juice for each of us."

"Coming right up," Mandy said, as the girls hurried off.

Elizabeth gave her sister a sideways glance. "I really don't believe you, Jess."

Jessica shrugged. "I don't see what you're making such a fuss about. You might as well enjoy all this attention, because by tomorrow everyone will have forgotten about what happened, and we'll be back to being average, everyday campers." She paused, frowning. "Well, maybe not average."

Elizabeth put her hand to her forehead. "I think I'm getting a real headache this time."

"You're such a stress case, Lizzie," Jessica told her, taking Elizabeth's hand off her forehead. "You really need to chill. I mean, we're OK, right? Nothing really bad happened, so what's to worry about?"

"I don't know," Elizabeth mumbled.

"Hey, maybe we could get Holly to let us take the day off," Jessica suggested. "Hang out in the cabin, munch out on the chocolate in our care packages, write letters to Mom and Dad—"

"I can't skip journalism," Elizabeth said, interrupting. "I'm way behind on my Roland Barge article.

I still haven't decided what part of his career to concentrate on."

Jessica held up her palms. "You find the stupidest things to worry about. I mean, what difference does it make? An author's an author, right?"

"Well, Roland Barge led a really unusual life," Elizabeth told her. "He was one of the greatest writers of his time, and—"

"—and he was absolutely charming as a young man."

Elizabeth looked up to see Gunnie standing by the table.

"So how are you doing, survivors? You gave us all quite a scare," Gunnie added.

Jessica quickly clutched Elizabeth's arm. "We're still a little shaken, Gunnie." She coughed. "But I think that after some breakfast and some free time, we'll be able to move on after this traumatic experience."

Gunnie looked at Jessica sternly. "You know, I'm tempted to give you a lecture about camp safety, Jessica, but I'm told Holly already took care of that."

Jessica nodded vigorously. "And believe me, Gunnie, she didn't need to. After what happened, I would never, ever, ever—"

"*Anyway*, Gunnie," Elizabeth said, interrupting again, unable to contain herself, "what were you saying about Roland Barge? Did you actually know him?"

Gunnie smiled and took a seat. "Certainly did. My uncle owned the property here, and I visited every summer. I was just a girl at the time. And, of course, that was before he changed his name."

Jessica's eyes sparked. "He changed his name? You mean like a movie star?"

"It *is* more common among movie stars than literary writers," Gunnie responded. "And I can't say I know why he did it. Perhaps he didn't think an author with the name Richard Bittle could sell books. It doesn't sound nearly as literary as Roland Barge."

Elizabeth gasped. "Richard Bittle?" she repeated.

"Roland Barge has a much nicer ring to it, doesn't it?" Gunnie went on. "I think he made a fine choice, too."

Elizabeth tried desperately to hide her discomfort. *It's just another coincidence*, she attempted to tell herself. *Richard* was definitely a common name. But what about *Bittle*? Where had it come from? Elizabeth was sure she had never met anyone with that last name.

"He kept his same initials but gave himself a more elegant-sounding name," Gunnie explained. "He always said he would rise far above the status of a servant. Richard Bittle was so daring and ambitious." She grinned at the memory.

"A servant?" Elizabeth repeated, her voice quavering slightly. *A servant—just like Amelia's Richard Bittle.*

"You know, I have this weird feeling I've heard the name *Richard Bittle* before," Jessica said, as she turned to Elizabeth. "Do we have a friend in Sweet Valley named Richard Bittle or something?"

Elizabeth bit her lip. Jessica obviously hadn't connected the two stories. *And for now, that's probably better.* "Um—Richard is one of Dad's friends at work, I think," she said quickly.

There has to be some explanation, Elizabeth thought, her mind racing. Maybe she had read about bits and pieces of his past in the old newspaper clippings and had unconsciously reconstructed them as her own plot. "Gunnie," she began cautiously, "the old articles written about him mentioned his original name, right?"

"Oh, no," Gunnie replied. "He never let anyone else find out that Roland Barge wasn't his real name. Only those who had known him in the manor were aware of the switch. It was never even mentioned in his biography and certainly not in any of the articles that were written about him over the years."

Elizabeth's heart was pounding—but she couldn't turn away from the truth. Somehow she needed to go on. "If you don't mind, Gunnie, maybe you can tell me a bit more. I need some information for my article. I'll even quote you as a source." Elizabeth removed a pad from her backpack.

Gunnie smiled pleasantly. "I love talking about the olden days. People rarely seem interested."

"Well, I'd like a bit of background first. What was your uncle's name?" Elizabeth asked.

"Patrick O'Neil," Gunnie replied.

Elizabeth felt her heart constrict. O'Neil Manor was the name of the estate that Amelia worked at! "Did he have a name for the land?" she asked nervously.

"O'Neil Manor," she said reverently.

"Really?" Elizabeth's voice shook.

"You didn't think it had always been called Camp Faraway, did you?" Gunnie asked, smiling.

"Well, no, I guess not." Elizabeth forced a tight smile. *What does it mean? Does the pen somehow know the past?*

"He never had any children, so he left me the property in his will," Gunnie told them. "When I decided to turn it into a camp, I was only able to keep the original stables and the theater. The rest was torn down. Of course, the natural wonders of the property have remained, Emerald Lake, the underground caves—"

"So tell us more about Roland," Jessica interrupted. "Was he handsome?"

"Oh, very. He was tall and dark." Gunnie looked wistful. "But what I remember most about Richard during the early days was that he was rather friendly with a kitchen girl."

"Kitchen girl?" Elizabeth repeated in a whisper.

Gunnie tapped her finger on the table. "Her name seems to have escaped me, but not her face. She was just beautiful."

Elizabeth could barely breathe. A beautiful kitchen girl—it had to be Amelia Champlain!

"Amelia!" Gunnie exclaimed suddenly. "That's it. Amelia Chaplin. No, Amelia Champlain. I haven't thought about her in years. Well, Amelia was a mysterious woman in her own right. She really broke Roland's heart."

"What do you mean?" Elizabeth asked.

"How could she dare break Roland's heart?" Jessica wanted to know. "I mean, he sounds like such a dream. What was her problem? Didn't she love him?"

"Oh, very much," Elizabeth murmured.

"What's that, dear?" Gunnie asked.

Elizabeth's face heated up. *Nice one, Elizabeth.* "I mean, she must have, right?" she said quickly.

"At one time it seemed that way," Gunnie said. "I remember seeing them take a rowboat on Emerald Lake on many occasions. She was truly enchanted by him. Then one day she left him a note that said she was running off with another man. He showed it to me. It was very cold and cruel. Richard was devastated."

"Poor Richard," Jessica said compassionately.

"I don't think he ever got over Amelia, either,"

Gunnie said. "I often thought that was why he grew to be such a bitter old man. He never loved again."

"But what about Amelia?" Elizabeth asked. "Did she become a writer, too?"

"Heavens, no. Amelia was just a kitchen girl," Gunnie said. "Whatever would make you think she'd become a writer?"

Elizabeth's face grew even hotter. "Oh, well, I guess I—"

"Who cares about whether or not she was a writer, anyway?" Jessica broke in. "What I want to know is, who'd she hook up with?"

"I never did find out about who had stolen her heart away from Richard. And no one ever heard from her again." Gunnie sighed.

"You're kidding." Elizabeth covered her mouth with her hand. "What do you think happened to her?"

Gunnie looked at the twins with a serious expression. "As I told you the first evening at the Welcome Bonfire, this land has a rich, complicated history. There are many legends associated with these grounds—and some murders."

Elizabeth gasped. "You think that Amelia was murdered?"

"When people disappear, murder is always a possibility," Gunnie said in a low voice.

"Oh, come on," Jessica protested with a laugh.

"Why do you have to be so gruesome. I bet Amelia just ran off with the gardener."

Gunnie smiled faintly. "That's also a possibility."

Elizabeth's heart was thundering in her ribs. If Amelia was murdered, would Jessica be in danger also?

One thing was sure—Elizabeth couldn't wait another moment to tell her sister everything.

Fourteen

◇

"I'm psyched we got out of going to swim class. I've had enough of that slimy lake for a while," Jessica said, as she and Elizabeth arrived back at the cabin after breakfast. "I think it might be damaging my hair."

Elizabeth sat down on her trunk and took a deep breath. "Jessica, there's something I need—"

"I think what we both need is a good deep-conditioning treatment," Jessica interrupted. "I have three hours before play rehearsal."

"Fine. But first—"

"First I'll get the chocolate." Jessica licked her lips.

"Jessica, I *really* need to talk to you," Elizabeth blurted out before Jessica could interrupt her again. She patted the spot on the trunk next to her. "You better sit down."

"Sheesh, well, why didn't you just say so?" Jessica grabbed her chocolate bar before plopping down beside her sister. "So what is it now?"

"Richard Bittle isn't one of Dad's colleagues," Elizabeth said.

Jessica held her palms up. "So what?"

"Let me start over." Elizabeth sighed. "Remember when I told you all about the details of the story I wrote with the pen?"

"Oh, right, the supernatural pen," Jessica teased.

"You may think that's funny, but the reason the name Richard Bittle sounded familiar to you is because that's the name of one of the characters." Elizabeth put her hands on Jessica's shoulders and looked her in the eye. "I think it's a true story."

Jessica furrowed her brow. "Did you hit your head on something when you were drowning in the lake? How could you be writing a true story?"

"I'm not really the author. The pen is," Elizabeth insisted.

"Don't tell me you're back to that crazy idea again." Jessica looked closely at her sister.

"It's not crazy!" Exasperated, Elizabeth stood up and reached underneath her mattress for the pad. "Want proof?" She flipped to the page where she had first written his name. "Here's the proof." She pointed to the slanted cursive that read *Richard Bittle*.

Jessica stared at the pad. "I don't get it," she

said, running her fingers over the name.

Elizabeth turned back to the first page. "There's more. Here I wrote about Amelia Champlain. She's a beautiful kitchen girl, just like Gunnie said."

"But how did you know?" Jessica asked. "Gunnie could hardly remember her name in the first place."

"That's exactly what I'm trying to explain. How could I have possibly known their names?" Elizabeth argued. "The pen brought me the information."

A glimmer of fear crossed Jessica's face.

"It gets even weirder." Elizabeth exhaled loudly. "Everything I've written so far with the pen has come true."

"That bizarre thing with the fireplace." Jessica gritted her teeth at the memory.

Elizabeth nodded guiltily. "And there's more. Night before last, the pen called for me. I can't really explain it, but I stayed up all night writing the next chapter. I mean, the pen told the story— it's like I just let it borrow my hand."

"What did it write this time?" Jessica asked.

Elizabeth wrung her hands. "That Amelia nearly drowned on Emerald Lake."

Jessica's jaw dropped.

"She was supposed to meet Richard in her boat one night, but he never showed up. While she was trying to row back to shore, she realized her boat had been ruptured with a knife. Amelia fell overboard when it filled up with water. There was a terrible storm. The only reason Amelia didn't drown was because some mysterious fisherman happened to notice her." She flipped the pages over. "You can read it all for yourself."

Jessica skimmed over the pages with her mouth agape. "It was another warning!"

"It didn't occur to me until you had already gone out on the lake alone," Elizabeth confessed, as tears started to pour from her eyes. "If I had realized that, nothing ever would have happened to you.

"Lizzie, it's OK. I'm OK. Nothing bad has happened," Jessica tried to reassure her.

"*Has* happened," Elizabeth repeated, wiping her eyes. "I'm just afraid that something is *going* to happen."

Jessica looked at Elizabeth fearfully. "What do you mean *something*?"

Elizabeth swallowed. "You heard what Gunnie said about Amelia, didn't you? No one ever saw her again. And everything—everything—that's happened to her so far has happened to you."

"Yeah." Jessica gazed thoughtfully into space before looking at her sister. "Maybe I'll have two gorgeous men fighting over me, and then I'll run off with the gardener."

"Jessica!" Elizabeth exclaimed. "How can you make a joke out of this?"

Jessica shrugged. "Why do you have to imagine the worst, Elizabeth? I'm sure there's a good explanation for this. I just know it."

Elizabeth buried her face in her hands. "Maybe we should get Mom and Dad to pick us up from camp tonight. It's the only way you'll be safe for sure."

"Are you out of your mind? I'm starring in a play in a few days," Jessica protested.

"But it's the only way out," Elizabeth told her. "I'll start packing. I'm sorry about the play. At least I'll have an excuse for never finishing my article on Roland Barge."

Jessica clutched her sister's arm. "That's it."

"What's it?" Elizabeth asked.

"Isn't it obvious? It has to do with your article. You read all that stuff about Roland, and something must have triggered you to write it," Jessica said triumphantly.

Elizabeth shook her head. "I know it's more than that, Jessica. I think the pen is trying to communicate something to me. I've felt that ever since I found it glowing in the cave." She began packing up her belongings.

Jessica grabbed the T-shirt her sister was folding. "You might as well save yourself the trouble, Elizabeth, because there's no way I'm leaving and giving up the acting role of the century."

Elizabeth looked at her sister in distress.

"What's a part when your life could be in danger?"

"You're just overreacting to some coincidences and stuff," Jessica argued.

"But two minutes ago you believed me!" Elizabeth wailed.

Jessica rolled her eyes. "I know. I can't believe you almost got me to go along with your twisted theory."

"I'm trying to protect you," Elizabeth said sternly.

"Oh fine," Jessica said sarcastically. "Let's just call Mom and tell her that we're having a blast at camp but you found this pen in a cave and it has warned us about all this stuff and now you think I might get murdered because a maid disappeared seventy years ago. I'm sure she'll just rush up to rescue us." Jessica shook her head.

Elizabeth bit her lip in frustration.

"You're acting really nutty, Elizabeth," Jessica continued. "You're taking your assignment too seriously, and it has somehow caused a brain malfunction." She walked across the cabin to her bag of cosmetics. "Now, if you don't mind, I'm conditioning my ends."

Fifteen

$\Diamond$

"'The fork goes here, the knife here, and the spoon here,'" Mandy said.

She and Jessica were seated at a regal dining room table on the stage. They were both in costume. Jessica had on an elegant, old-fashioned evening gown and dangling rhinestone earrings. Mandy wore a short dark wig, a little mustache, and a tuxedo.

"'The napkin is placed on your lap before even a drop of water is sipped,'" Mandy continued. She handed Jessica a cloth napkin.

As Jessica reached for the napkin, one of her earrings accidentally fell off. It landed in her lap, and she quickly clipped it back on.

"'Speaking of water . . .'" Jessica picked up the water glass and guzzled it. She wiped her mouth with the back of her hand. In the process, she knocked off the earring into the glass. "'Boy, does that hit the spot, Prince Joseph.'"

Mandy looked horrified. "'Not like that. Like this.'" Mandy lifted her own water glass and took a small sip. When she put the glass down, her mustache was sticking to it.

"Oops," she said under her breath as she reattached the mustache.

"'Now let's try your walking exercises. A real princess has a delicate posture.'" Mandy stood up, sticking out her chest and throwing her head back. Her wig dropped off. When she put it back on, it was upside down and hanging in her eyes. A tiny giggle escaped her lips.

Jessica glanced out into the audience. Priscilla was positively smirking. Miranda was having trouble keeping a straight face.

But Jessica refused to let a few kinks get in the way of finishing the scene. She began to stand up, but her dress was caught under the leg of the chair. She tugged at it. Finally the dress released, but the chair toppled over, hit the table, and threw the candelabra and place settings to the ground. The glasses shattered.

Suddenly the auditorium filled with hysterical laughter. Even Gunnie was pursing her lips to keep from laughing.

Jessica felt her cheeks flush. "Should we, um, take it from the top?"

"Let's clean up this mess, first," Gunnie said. "You just have to get comfortable in your costumes," she added patiently. "This is why we have a dress rehearsal."

"I'd like to go back to the library, if you don't mind," Elizabeth said to Lisa in journalism class.

Elizabeth had decided to forget her worries about Jessica for the afternoon and to catch up on her article. Somehow the daylight was a comfort to her—the scary events never seemed to strike until evening. If she could find out more about Roland Barge, she might discover an unexpected clue and figure out what was really going on.

Lisa looked up from a paper she was editing. "You've spent an awful lot of time compiling research for your article, Elizabeth. I appreciate your thoroughness, but I'd like to see some work from you now."

Elizabeth blushed. "Yeah, well, um, Rome wasn't built in a day," she said sheepishly.

"And good journalists never use clichés," Lisa replied lightly. "Most of the girls have already turned in rough drafts of their stories."

"I promise you, I'll have something for you before the deadline," Elizabeth said.

"I sure hope so. You were so excited about the article," Lisa recalled. "Roland Barge was an influential author, Elizabeth. It should be thrilling for you to learn about him."

Suddenly Elizabeth had a flash of insight "Right. And I'm missing one important part of the story, Lisa. How can I write about a great author if I've never read one of his books?"

Elizabeth arrived in the library and searched around for the fiction section. She scanned the shelf until she found the row of Roland Barge novels. *The Ghost of Mr. Green*, *Skeleton Island*, and *The Attic Door* were prominently displayed. Elizabeth sighed, frustrated. The title she was looking for was missing Elizabeth was walking back to her desk when something caught her eye. An old red book with a scuffed, frazzled binding sat on a nearby shelf. Its title had worn away.

Elizabeth climbed up a rickety ladder and reached for the book. Her hand shook as she slowly opened the cover. Bold black letters read *Death of a Hangman*. A week ago, the thought of reading the book had terrified her. But Elizabeth knew that examining the book could only offer her insight into Roland Barge—and maybe Amelia Champlain, too And then there was the undeniable connection of having found the pen in the cave—where the man in the novel was hung. Maybe, just maybe, it would give her a new lead.

She sat down in a big cozy chair by the window

and began to read. Elizabeth was immediately drawn into the book. It told the story of an evil murderer who buried the bodies of his victims in a cave. Elizabeth's arms were covered with goose bumps. She looked up at the librarian, just to get the sense that she was not alone. She couldn't remember ever having read a book that was so creepy. *But I have to go on reading,* she told herself. *I have to.*

As the story progressed, the murderer mysteriously disappeared, and a search party set out to find him. In the end, he was recovered in the cave, hanging from a rope. He had been detained by the spirits of those he had murdered.

Elizabeth slammed the book closed and put it back on the shelf. The story was gripping, terrifying—but what did it have to do with the life of Roland Barge, or the life of Amelia Champlain? Was there something, anything, between the lines of the novel?

Elizabeth shook her head. She was at a loss.

The real answers would have to come from the pen.

"Ready for rehearsal?" Miranda asked Jessica in Windelwisp that evening after dinner.

"I need to curl my hair first," Jessica replied, examining the ends of her blond ponytail. "I told Gunnie I would show her how I'm going to wear it for the show. After today's awful run-through, I want to make sure that I'm perfect tonight." Jessica began rolling her hair up in the steaming rollers that were waiting on her trunk.

"Well, I can't be late, Jess. My scene's up first tonight," Miranda told her.

"You and Mandy go ahead without me," Jessica said. "I'll just be a few extra minutes."

"Try an hour," Elizabeth teased. "Jessica takes forever when she's primping."

"Do not," Jessica retorted.

"See you in the auditorium," Miranda said, as she and Mandy left.

As Jessica rolled up another lock of hair, she felt Elizabeth's eyes boring into her. "Not that I don't want your company, Elizabeth, but aren't you a little bored just sitting there? Don't you have something to do? Like maybe hang out with Starr in the lounge?"

"I think I'll just hang out here, Jess," Elizabeth replied.

"You're not still obsessing over your mystery pen, are you?" Jessica asked incredulously.

"I need to go on with the story," Elizabeth explained. "I need to make sure that you're safe here."

"Not that again!" Jessica rolled her eyes.

"I have to find out if Amelia was murdered," Elizabeth continued.

"Please!" Jessica exclaimed. "I already gave

you a brilliant theory. Amelia ran off with the gardener, and they lived happily ever after. Or maybe it was that gorgeous fisherman who rescued her on the lake. I'm sure Amelia wasn't exactly thrilled about being a maid. They may have moved across the country or something to get better jobs. And it wasn't as easy to keep in touch in those days. It's not like everyone had a telephone, you know."

"I wish I could believe you." Elizabeth sighed as she climbed up the bunk.

"Believe me, Elizabeth, when we're home in Sweet Valley next week, you're going to realize what a lunatic you're being." Jessica took out one roller and turned to her sister. "But more important, how do the curls look?"

"Gorgeous," Elizabeth said indifferently.

Jessica smiled confidently in the small mirror. "I'm going to look too pretty to get murdered, that's for sure."

Elizabeth watched her sister run down the pathway to her rehearsal. She tapped the pen on the pad nervously, afraid of what the story might tell her. *Well, here goes.* She put the pen to the paper and let the rest of the story unfold.

Amelia came into the kitchen with bundles of freshly picked greens from the garden. There, in its usual place by the copper pots and pans, was a sealed note from Richard. She opened the letter and read his adoring words.

> Amelia, my love,
>   Perhaps we should stay away from the lake. Instead, I thought we'd meet for an evening stroll through the cave on the far end of the property. I count the moments until I see you.
>   With love and adoration,
>   Richard

Amelia thought an evening stroll through the cave sounded less than inviting, but she had no way to suggest a change of plans. He had probably already left to meet her. And Richard will protect me, she thought, as she set out to meet her darling.

As Amelia hiked toward the cave, her heart beat with anticipation. This is the night. I just know it. This is the night we are to be engaged. The night we will form an eternal bond.

Amelia reached the dark mouth of the cave and stepped inside wearily. She tripped on a bump in the ground and stumbled a few feet. "Richard? Richard, are you in here?"

Her words echoed through the cavernous space.

"Down here, my love," Richard replied.

"But I can hardly see," she cried. "Please come up to the entrance and help me."

"There's nothing to be afraid of, Amelia," he insisted, his tone slightly menacing.

Amelia was startled by his lack of compassion. "I'm afraid I might fall," she explained. "Please come to me, or I'll have to leave."

"Then, fine, let me help you," he said.

Amelia sighed with relief as she waited for Richard. She heard his footsteps and finally saw the glow of his white shirt.

She moved toward him with opened arms. "Oh, Richard," she said. "Of all the places to meet, why here? Why at night?"

"Because it's isolated. No one can see us," he said. "It's like our own world, my darling."

Amelia sighed. When he put it that way, it was wonderfully romantic.

Richard moved toward her for an embrace. Amelia held on to his waist and rested her head on his shoulder. This is all I need to get through life, she thought dreamily. Her books and great ambitions were secondary to her feelings for Richard Bittle.

"Amelia?" Richard asked.

"Yes?" she replied eagerly.

He broke their embrace and rubbed her cheek with the back of his hand.

"What is it, Richard?" she asked.

Richard suddenly reached for her throat. Amelia choked as she struggled to be released.

"Richard! Richard!" she gagged, using all her

strength to break away from his hold.

Richard laughed wickedly as he applied more pressure to her frail neck.

Elizabeth threw down the pen in horror. Her palms were sweating. *Why Richard?* Elizabeth asked herself. Amelia had loved him so dearly. Why would he want to hurt her?

Elizabeth stood up. As much as she wanted—needed—to know the rest of the story, she was afraid to be alone. She couldn't finish writing without Jessica at her side.

Elizabeth's hands were shaking uncontrollably. If it really were true that Jessica's and Amelia's lives were becoming mirror images, Jessica could be in for some trouble. *At least I know that Jessica is safe at rehearsal with everybody*, she assured herself, as she shoved the pen in her pocket, grabbed the notepad, and headed off toward the theater arts building to find her sister.

Sixteen

◇

"'These hands have never touched the soil. I refuse to be shipped off to some wretched farm and take on the life of a pauper.'"

When Elizabeth came into the theater, Miranda was on stage rehearsing a scene with Mandy. Elizabeth gazed into the audience, searching for Jessica. *Where is she?*

Gunnie was seated in her director's chair, watching the actors perform. Elizabeth strode over to her.

"Gunnie, I need to speak to Jessica," Elizabeth said.

"Shhhh!" Gunnie scolded. "We're in the middle of a run-through, Elizabeth. You should know better."

"Is she backstage?" Elizabeth went on in a raised voice.

Gunnie shooed her away. "Mandy, you're not enunciating clearly enough," she called.

As Elizabeth glanced around the auditorium again, her heart began thumping furiously. "Gunnie, where's Jessica?" she repeated fearfully.

"And Miranda, you need to look out into the audience," Gunnie continued.

Suddenly, Elizabeth was overcome with fear and dread. *"Why won't you tell me where Jessica is?"*

The room silenced. Everyone stared at Elizabeth, whose face had turned beet red.

Gunnie finally acknowledged her. "Your sister is late, Elizabeth." She tapped her wristwatch angrily. "I'm afraid she's not taking her responsibilities as an actor seriously."

"But—but that's impossible," Elizabeth sputtered. "I mean, she left for rehearsal over an hour ago."

"I guess she must be playing hooky," Priscilla called from the back. "She's probably over in the lodge hanging out with the others."

"You're wrong," Elizabeth insisted. "She was on her way here."

"Jessica never would have skipped out on rehearsal," Miranda agreed.

Suddenly, Elizabeth felt as though all the breath were being sucked out of her. One explanation was racing through her mind—one horrible, unspeakable explanation. "Gunnie!" she exclaimed, grabbing the older woman's arm. "You have to come to Hangman's Cave with me."

Gunnie frowned. "Whatever for? I prohibit going into that cave at night."

"Gunnie—I know it sounds crazy, but Jessica's life is in danger," she whispered frantically. "Gunnie, please, you have to listen to me," Elizabeth begged.

"Everybody take five," Gunnie announced to her students.

"What's going on, Elizabeth?" Miranda yelled from the stage.

"I don't have time to explain," Elizabeth replied, grabbing Gunnie's hand and dragging her out of the theater.

"Slow down, Elizabeth, and tell me what's going on," Gunnie demanded once they were outside.

"I'll tell you on the way to Hangman's Cave. But please, Gunnie, we have to hurry," Elizabeth pleaded. "It's a matter of life and death."

A dark shadow crossed Gunnie's face. "All right. Let's go."

Elizabeth raced through the brush on the way to Hangman's Cave, Gunnie close hehind her. Shaking with panic, Elizabeth did her best to retell the story to Gunnie along the way.

"It has to do with Richard Bittle and Amelia Champlain," Elizabeth began. "It all started when I found an antique red pen in a crevice of the cave. When I decided to write with it, it just took me over."

Gunnie frowned. "Elizabeth, maybe writing that article about Roland Barge has gotten the best of you."

"I know it sounds crazy, but you have to believe me. I've never exaggerated about anything before," Elizabeth told her.

"All right. Go on," Gunnie said dubiously.

"Well, I meant to use the pen to write my article—but instead I ended up composing this spooky story. It was like the pen had a power all its own—like my hand was just a tool for it to write a story," Elizabeth said.

Gunnie pursed her lips. "But what does this have to do with the cave—or with Jessica?"

Elizabeth took a deep breath. "The story that the pen has been writing is the true story about Richard Bittle and Amelia Champlain. And the scariest part of all of this is that everything that happened to Amelia in the story has happened to Jessica, too."

"What do you mean? What happened to Amelia?" Gunnie asked, struggling to keep up with Elizabeth.

Elizabeth looked into Gunnie's eyes even as she hurried forward. "What happened to Jessica on the lake last night also happened to Amelia in the story."

Suddenly Gunnie gasped. "And in actuality. Elizabeth, Amelia nearly drowned on the lake during a storm in real life as well. She was rescued by a fisherman."

Elizabeth was having difficulty breathing—and not just from moving so quickly. "It really is like the pen tells the past—and the future, too. And that means—" Elizabeth trailed off, too horrified to continue.

"That means what, Elizabeth?" Gunnie pressed, suddenly recognizing the gravity of the situation. "What more is there to the story?"

"Richard had told Amelia to meet him in the cave," Elizabeth went on hoarsely. "And when she got there, he started to strangle her." Suddenly a sob escaped her mouth. "Oh, Gunnie, I'm so afraid that—"

"There's a shortcut up ahead," Gunnie said, cutting through an open field. "We'll make it."

Elizabeth and Gunnie were panting when they arrived at the mouth of the cave. Gunnie grabbed the miniature flashlight from her belt buckle and they bolted inside. She shined the light along the textured walls and floors.

There was no trace of Jessica, or anyone else.

Suddenly, Elizabeth heard something in the distance—a low, awful moan. "I think that's Jessica," she cried desperately.

"Aughhhhh!" echoed lightly throughout the space.

"Jessica!" Gunnie called out. "Are you in here?"

"Jess! It's me!" Elizabeth hollered. "We're going to rescue you."

"Aughhhhh!" echoed through the cave again.

"We've got to find her!" Elizabeth shrieked.

Gunnie and Elizabeth scurried for the steel railing that led to the lower level of the cave. Elizabeth slipped and clutched the rail with all her might to avoid tumbling over. As they descended, the moaning became louder.

Elizabeth cupped her hand to her ear. "It's Jessica, Gunnie, I just know it."

Finally, they made it down to the pool of water at the bottom. Gunnie lit up the water with her flashlight, then dragged it along the caverns. But Jessica was nowhere in sight.

"What do we do?" Elizabeth asked in a panic.

A bloodcurdling scream resounded in the air. It sent shock waves through Elizabeth's body, and suddenly she was unable to move or think.

"This way," Gunnie instructed, moving on. "Hurry."

The sound of moaning suddenly ceased.

Elizabeth couldn't find her voice. *What if we're too late? What if—* Then she shook her head. She wouldn't give up—she *couldn't* leave the cave without her sister. "We're coming, Jess. Just hang on!"

Elizabeth followed Gunnie through the maze of caverns. She tripped on a bump and fell to the floor. As she pulled herself up, she saw a school of bats hovering overhead. One swooped down and brushed along the side of her arm. She cringed but ran on.

"Jessica, where are you?" Elizabeth cried, as she turned the corner.

Up against the far end of the wall, Jessica was cowering, her hands clutching her throat.

Elizabeth ran for her sister and grabbed her.

Jessica began gasping and sobbing. "I thought I was . . . I thought I was going to die." Her lips quivered.

"Oh, Jess," Elizabeth said, sobbing.

The sisters hugged tightly.

"You saved me, Elizabeth," Jessica said, not letting go. "I—I've never been so scared in my whole entire life."

"We're here now. Everything is going to be OK," Elizabeth said, attempting to calm her sister.

"Are you all right, dear?" Gunnie asked soothingly, trying to catch her breath. "Tell us what happened."

Jessica wiped the tears from her eyes. "It felt like two big hands were wrapped around my throat. I—I was being choked. I couldn't get away."

"Oh, Jess, I'm so sorry. I never should have let you out of the cabin alone," Elizabeth told her. "It was a huge mistake."

"I was screaming at the top of my lungs, but nobody heard me. I thought I would never make it out alive. How did you know I was in here?" Jessica sniffled.

Elizabeth looked at her sister. "It was the pen, Jess," she said softly.

"The pen?" Jessica repeated weakly, her eyes brimming with tears.

Elizabeth nodded. "Amelia had received a love note to meet Richard here for an evening stroll. But when she arrived, he attacked her. Once I got to that part, I was so scared, I had to stop writing. I didn't realize that your life was in danger until I got to the theater and you weren't there."

Jessica's whole body shook with sobs. "I should have listened to you. I'm so sorry, Lizzie."

Gunnie put an arm around each girl. "But there's a missing piece. How did you end up in the cave in the first place?"

Jessica shook her head, perplexed. "I was on my way to play rehearsal. Something pulled me toward here. I can't explain it." She put her face in her hands.

"Let's get out of here and try to make some sense of this." Gunnie motioned the girls toward her.

Elizabeth's hand felt a sudden surge of electricity. "We can't leave yet. The pen is calling for me."

"What's calling—?" Gunnie began.

Elizabeth's fingers trembled as she pulled the pen from her pocket. It was glowing so brightly, it was almost blinding. Gunnie shielded her eyes.

"Just wait," Elizabeth pleaded. "We may still be in danger."

Jessica clung to Gunnie.

Elizabeth uncapped the pen and stood close to a wall of the cave. She placed the pen on the wall's surface, and it began writing in its ornate cursive. As her hand moved, Elizabeth stared straight into Gunnie's eyes.

Gunnie drew in a breath as Elizabeth's hand went still. Elizabeth stepped back and began to read the words.

"Richard killed me," she read aloud from the wall. "He lured me to the cave with promises of love. He tried to strangle me, then he drowned me in the bottomless pool. All so he could steal my art, my dream."

Elizabeth turned to her sister, her heart pounding. "That's it!"

Jessica went pale. "Oh, my gosh!"

Gunnie was gazing at the slanted cursive with a frown. "I'm afraid I don't understand."

Elizabeth stared at her intently. "You were right when you guessed that Amelia's disappearance indicated murder. But what we never expected was that *Richard* was the murderer!"

Gunnie gasped.

"He tried to kill her on the lake, but when he failed there, he had to lure her into the cave to do the deed. He was plotting to steal Amelia's manuscripts all along," Elizabeth explained.

Gunnie looked startled. "What do you mean—*Amelia's* manuscripts?"

"Amelia was a wonderful writer, Gunnie," Elizabeth said softly. "And Roland Barge was—Roland Barge was a plagiarizer!"

Gunnie gazed from the cursive on the cave wall to Elizabeth's face. "You mean—you mean all of the books by Roland Barge weren't written by Roland at all, but by Amelia Champlain?"

Elizabeth nodded. "Richard saw Amelia's talent and devotion. He was always encouraging her and praising her, but—"

"But all the time, he was trying to steal her material," Jessica finished, her voice trembling. "And he had to kill her to do it."

"Amelia must have dropped the pen on the floor during the final struggle," Elizabeth went on. "That's why her soul stayed in it."

"Her soul—?" Gunnie murmured.

Elizabeth pointed to the wall. "The pen is Amelia's way of telling us the truth about what happened to her."

Gunnie's lips were quivering. "I just never would have suspected Richard. He seemed so in love with Amelia."

"Well, it's time that people knew the truth about Roland Barge—and about Amelia Champlain,"

Elizabeth said. "It's time for her to be appreciated as the real literary genius."

Gunnie frowned. "Roland Barge was a revered author, Elizabeth. You can't expose anything without proof. We'll need to find the original manuscripts. Otherwise, it's no more than a theory. You could be accused of fabricating the story."

Elizabeth bit her lip. "I guess you're right. No one would—"

"The pen, Lizzie!" Jessica broke in. "The pen will tell us where they are."

Elizabeth looked at her sister and then at the glowing red pen in her hand. "Of course," she whispered. "The pen."

Elizabeth stood close to wall and put her hand back against its surface. *Tell me, Amelia,* she pleaded to the pen, *where are your manuscripts hidden?*

Her hand began to move along the wall in elaborate cursive.

Look under the old stable. There you will find my precious works, the pen scribbled out.

Seventeen

◇

"This way," Gunnie said to the twins as they emerged from the dark cave.

Elizabeth and Jessica scurried along quickly, making their way to the old stable on the other side of the campground.

"What now?" Jessica asked, looking around at the horses, wooden gates, and stacks of hay.

"It said *under* it," Elizabeth recalled. "Amelia's manuscripts must be hidden under the floorboards." She looked around until she noticed a loose wooden strip. "Over here!"

Gunnie reached down and yanked at the board. "Grab on, girls."

Elizabeth and Jessica clutched onto the loose board.

"When I count to three, let's give it a strong pull," Gunnie instructed.

The twins nodded.

"One." Everyone gulped. "Two." They exhaled. "Three." They pulled with all their might. The board released from the ground, and the girls stumbled all the way back to the stacks of hay.

Jessica ran back to the opening. "There they are!" she shrieked, pointing to some papers sticking out.

Elizabeth leaned in and began removing bundles of papers. "*Death of a Hangman*," she read off the title page. "*The Attic Door*," she read off another. "They're all of Amelia's novels."

Elizabeth handed the stack to Gunnie. Altogether, there were a dozen titles previously attributed to Roland Barge.

"And look," Elizabeth cried. "They're written in the same handwriting that came through from the pen."

Elizabeth ran her fingers over a page of cursive writing. The ink on the page was bluish lavender, just like the red pen's ink.

"Wow," Jessica marveled.

Gunnie stared at the pages. "And I thought that Amelia was just a pretty face."

"That was part of Richard's plot, too," Elizabeth explained. "He forbade her to talk to anyone about her literary aspirations. That way no one ever even suspected his foul play."

"These originals must be valuable," Gunnie

murmured. "We'll display them in the Faraway Library."

"Hey, look! There's more down here," Elizabeth said, digging in underneath. She retrieved handfuls of loose pages covered with messy black writing.

Gunnie perused the contents. "Looks like these were aborted attempts at writing novels of his own."

"Of course," Elizabeth said. "The publishers were counting on him to make them money. Once he ran out of Amelia's novels, he had to try to write one."

"But he was grossly untalented," Gunnie noted, looking down at a page.

Elizabeth noticed a completed manuscript. "Wait. This one he did have published. *Death on a Mountain Top.*" Elizabeth pointed to the title. "I read a review of this. The publishers thought that Roland Barge was such a big name that people would buy anything he wrote. But this book was a disaster. It never sold more than a few copies."

"And that's about the time he became reclusive," Gunnie recalled.

"What's this?" Jessica asked, fishing out a weathered composition pad.

Gunnie skimmed through it, too quickly for the girls to see. After a few moments, she looked up. "It's his journal."

"His journal?" Elizabeth repeated.

"It tells of his relationship with Amelia—and it gives all the details, every step of his plot," Gunnie realized.

"Read it, Gunnie," Jessica pleaded.

The girls sat on the haystack and listened intently as Gunnie read the tale in her deep mystical voice. The journal included information about how Richard had courted Amelia, and how he had fooled her into believing that her most prized manuscript had ignited in the fireplace. When Amelia was making tea, he hid the novel in his leather satchel and left the title page in the fire to mislead her.

"And you called me crazy," Elizabeth said to her sister. "The fact that your script burned—that was another clue to the puzzle!" Everything she had questioned was falling into place.

Gunnie continued reading from Roland's journal. It included an account of his attempt to kill Amelia on the lake by sabotaging her boat and finally ended with Amelia's dying words that her name would be vindicated.

"Ahhh, this looks interesting, girls. Listen up." Gunnie cleared her throat and read on. " 'Many years have passed, but the memory of Amelia has not escaped me. I am tortured by what I have done. I murdered the woman I loved to gain literary acclaim, but what for? I am no longer a revered author, I have become a lonely, evil man. I will go back to the cave to pay homage to Amelia's spirit. I will stand at the spot by the pool where Amelia took her last breath. 'Oh, Amelia, darling Amelia, please forgive me. Without you I am nothing. I will join your spirit, so we can be together again.'"

Gunnie closed the journal and put it down. "That's where it ends. It reads to me like a suicide note."

Elizabeth nodded. "It sounds like he went to the cave and drowned himself in the bottomless pool," she said softly.

"There were many speculations about the disappearance of Roland Barge—and now it looks like we have the truth," Gunnie said.

"What a sad story!" Jessica exclaimed.

Elizabeth looked down at the pen in her hand. The glow had disappeared, and it no longer felt alive in her fingers. "Amelia can finally rest in peace," she said with a satisfied sigh.

Gunnie looked at the twins appreciatively. "I always knew there were a lot of spooky legends about this place. I just never knew they were true."

Eighteen

$\diamond$

"I think you should keep the pen," Gunnie said to Elizabeth, as she walked the twins back to Windelwisp.

It had been a rough night and Gunnie and the girls were covered with mud, hay, and scratches.

Elizabeth looked at Gunnie quizzically. "I was planning to bring it back to the cave. I thought I could leave it in the exact spot where I originally found it."

"Don't be silly, Elizabeth. You earned it," Gunnie insisted.

"And I bet Amelia would want you to have it. After all, it's thanks to you that the truth about her will come out." Jessica wiped dirt from her cheek. "Besides, do you really want to go back in that cave again? Because if you do, you're on your own. I've seen enough of that spooky place."

"Just take it, dear. I hope you'll cherish it for years," Gunnie remarked.

Elizabeth clutched the pen in her hands. It was a wonderful treasure and a better memento of camp than the Faraway sweatshirts everyone else had planned to buy. "Thank you, Gunnie. I'll take good care of it." She slipped the pen back into her pocket, then smiled at Gunnie. "And Gunnie?"

"Yes, dear?"

"I also wanted to thank you for trusting me," Elizabeth said. "I never could have saved Jessica without you."

Gunnie smiled. "And I have to thank you. I must say, after forty years of running Camp Faraway, this has been my most memorable session, because of you two."

"You're back!" Mandy exclaimed as the twins stepped inside the cabin.

"Where have you been all night?" Starr asked, rushing up to them. "Rolling around in the dirt or something?"

Elizabeth glanced at Jessica. Somehow she wasn't in the mood to tell the whole spooky story.

"Oh, nothing much," Jessica said nonchalantly. "We were just hanging out with Gunnie."

"Right," Elizabeth confirmed. "Just shooting the breeze." She sat down and pulled off her shoes.

Miranda frowned. "You started screaming in the

theater just so you could shoot the breeze?"

Mandy raised an eyebrow at Jessica. "And you skipped rehearsal just so you could hang out?"

"I thought you said you were staying in to work on your article, Elizabeth," Starr added.

Elizabeth met eyes with her sister. "Actually, I was just doing a little extra research. My article on Roland Barge is going to be absolutely amazing!"

"And now I'd like some of you to read your work out loud," Lisa told her students.

"Lisa?" Elizabeth raised her hand.

"Let me guess—you have to go to the library?" Lisa said.

"I have an article to write," Elizabeth explained. "I won't be able to get it done if you're all working on something out loud."

"OK, Elizabeth, go do your stuff," Lisa conceded.

Elizabeth eagerly dashed out of the classroom. She walked along Emerald Lake, constructing the article in her mind.

Elizabeth took a seat at an old wooden table in the corner of the library. She pulled the red pen from her backpack and moved her finger along its textured surface. She was about to write the greatest article of her life. "The Truth About Roland Barge" was the title she had in mind.

Elizabeth flipped through her pad for a clean sheet of paper and began to write. Now that

Amelia's spirit was at rest, the pen no longer had any special powers. It was nothing more than a tool for Elizabeth's expression. But once Elizabeth got to work, the article seemed to write itself, anyway. Elizabeth had thought so long and hard about the story that it really was bursting to come out.

Elizabeth filled up page after page. Her head was full of so much information she seemed incapable of writing fast enough. She wrote about Amelia Champlain and O'Neil Manor. She even excerpted passages from Roland Barge's poorly written manuscripts. When she finished, she reread the article and checked for punctuation and spelling errors. As far as she could tell, it was ready for submission.

"So let's see it!"

Elizabeth turned around, startled. "Hi, Jess."

Jessica was standing over her shoulder, a big smile on her face. "So? Can I read it?"

Elizabeth raised an eyebrow. "You really want to read my article? It doesn't mention Johnny Buck, fall fashions, or anything like that."

Jessica put her hands on her hips. "Don't all writers need a good fact checker?" she asked.

"You never read my material for the *Sixers*," Elizabeth pointed out.

"This is kind of different, don't you think? Plus, I need to make sure you don't leave anything juicy out."

Elizabeth gave the handwritten pages to Jessica and watched eagerly as she read the story. Jessica seemed engrossed by the words and finally looked up at her sister when she had finished.

"You couldn't have possibly told it better, Lizzie," Jessica exclaimed.

"Sure you're not biased?" Elizabeth asked.

"You are a *brilliant* writer," Jessica insisted. "This is the coolest article I've ever read."

"Thanks, Jess," Elizabeth said, smiling. "I just hope Lisa thinks so, too."

"Well, Elizabeth, you've certainly been an interesting student," Lisa told her, looking up from Elizabeth's article.

Elizabeth was standing by Lisa's desk after class, and her stomach was doing flip-flops.

"And frankly," Lisa continued, "I didn't know what to expect after what we've been through, waiting for your article, your relentless research methods . . ."

Elizabeth bit her lip. "Do you think it's—acceptable?"

"Acceptable?" Lisa repeated calmly. "Actually, I think it's a good deal more than acceptable. I think it's a groundbreaking piece."

Elizabeth's eyes lit up. "You do?"

"Your dedication has definitely paid off," Lisa added. "'The Truth About Roland Barge' will be the cover story on the latest edition of *The Camp Faraway Gazette,* that's for sure."

* * *

"Bravo! Bravo!" The auditorium thundered with applause as the audience gave a standing ovation to the cast of *The Royal Switch.*

Jessica stood between Miranda and Mandy as they held hands and bowed together for the third time. *Whoever would have guessed we had such disastrous rehearsals?* Jessica thought. The production had been flawless. Jessica had never felt so confident, and she knew she had radiated on stage. Miranda had been completely convincing as Eleanor, Mandy's interpretation as Joseph had gotten endless laughs, and even Priscilla had given a nice performance.

Jessica looked out to the crowd and met eyes with her mother, father, and brother. They had taken the five-hour trip up to camp to see Jessica's debut.

"Time to take your solo bow," Miranda whispered as she and Mandy pushed Jessica to the front.

"Bravo, Bravo!" yelled someone from the wings.

Elizabeth suddenly appeared on stage and rushed to Jessica with a dozen long-stemmed roses.

"For you, Your Highness Penelope," Elizabeth told her sister.

"Thanks, Lizzie!" Jessica gave her sister an enormous hug before taking her final bow.

Elizabeth and Jessica walked along Emerald Lake on their way back to Windelwisp. Mr. Wakefield would meet them there with the station wagon, and Steven would help cart out the trunks.

"I'll miss Miranda so much. Wouldn't she be a perfect Unicorn?" Jessica asked. "I wish she'd move to Sweet Valley."

Elizabeth nodded. "I'll miss Starr, too. But I guess we can write letters and stuff."

"She'll probably write you poems," Jessica mused.

"Maybe she can come and visit us sometime," Elizabeth said.

"I wish the whole camp could come visit us," Jessica said wistfully.

Elizabeth looked at her sister skeptically. "The *whole* camp?"

Jessica giggled. "Well, maybe not everyone. I think I can deal with not seeing Priscilla Westover again. And with not being woken up by Gunnie every morning with that obnoxious bugle! But besides that, I'll miss just about everything."

Elizabeth breathed in the cool mountain air. She looked toward Emerald Lake. The sun shone down on its surface, reflecting a bright, shiny glare. A breeze in the air rustled the leaves on the trees, and the clear sky made the mountains visible. "Yeah, I'll miss everything, too. This is the most beautiful place on earth."

"Maybe Mom and Dad will let us come back next year," Jessica said.

"Maybe someday we could be counselors," Elizabeth added hopefully.

"You could be the journalism teacher, like Lisa," Jessica said. "I'll take everybody on the tour of

Hangman's Cave and give them all the gory details we discovered."

At the mention of the cave, Elizabeth felt a little chill run up her spine—she was spooked, but exhilarated, too. Maybe she hadn't written a mystery, as she had planned, but she had solved one of the greatest and oldest literary mysteries ever. Her discovery would be told about for years to come.

Elizabeth turned to her sister. "You can stick to running the acting workshops. The cave tour is my territory. It's my story to tell."

OK, Johnny, back where you belong, Jessica thought, as she pulled her Johnny Buck poster from her trunk. The twins had been home for a day, but Jessica wasn't interested in unpacking the rest of her stuff. She was sick of all her summer clothes anyway and couldn't wait to go to the mall to check out the new back-to-school fashions.

As she was tacking the poster on her bedroom wall, the phone rang.

"Hello?" Jessica said into the receiver.

"Bonjour," the voice on the other end replied.

"Lila!" Jessica exclaimed. "You're back!"

"Oui, oui," Lila said. "I had ze most magnifique time in Europe."

Jessica giggled. "Well, you won't believe what I—"

"Jessica!" Elizabeth appeared in Jessica's doorway, holding the *Sweet Valley Tribune.*

Jessica put her hand over the receiver. "Elizabeth, I'm talking to Lila. Can't we read the newspaper some other time?"

"But Jess, we're famous!" Elizabeth exclaimed. "Look! Here's my Roland Barge article, reprinted on the front page!"

"Your Roland Barge article!" Jessica repeated, amazed.

"*Roland Barge?*" Lila echoed in her French accent. "*Qui is Roland Barge?*"

"And that's not all," Elizabeth continued, flipping to the entertainment section. "There's a rave review of you in the play. It says you were the star and that your next stop will probably be Broadway!"

Jessica screamed, dropped the phone on the floor, and threw her arms around her sister. "I'm a star, I'm a star, I'm a star!"

"Hey, what's going on over there?" Lila's voice floated up from the receiver. Suddenly, she'd lost her French accent. "Jessica, what are you doing?"

The twins laughed, and Jessica picked up the receiver. "Sorry, Lila, but I've become a star over the summer!"

"What are you talking about, Jessica?" Lila asked, sounding irritated. "I thought you guys were just hanging out in boring old Sweet Valley this summer."

"Lila," Jessica said. "I had ze most magnifique summer ever!"

We hope you enjoyed reading this book. If you would like to receive further information about available titles in the Bantam series, just write to the address below, with your name and address:

Kim Prior
Bantam Books
61–63 Uxbridge Road
Ealing
London W5 5SA.

If you live in Australia or New Zealand and would like more information about the series, please write to:

Sally Porter
Transworld Publishers
(Australia) Pty Ltd
15–25 Helles Avenue
Moorebank
NSW 2170
AUSTRALIA

Kiri Martin
Transworld Publishers (NZ) Ltd
3 William Pickering Drive
Albany
Auckland
NEW ZEALAND

Created by FRANCINE PASCAL

Follow the adventures of Jessica, Elizabeth and all their friends at Sweet Valley as twelve-year-olds. A super series with one new title every month!

Hang out with the coolest kids around!

THE UNICORN CLUB

Jessica and Elizabeth Wakefield are just two of the terrific members of The Unicorn Club you've met in *Sweet Valley Twins* books. Now get to know some of their friends even better!

A sensational new *Sweet Valley* series.